DEAD AT MIDNIGHT

DEAD AT MIDNIGHT

WELCOME TO DEAD HOUSE™ BOOK THREE

M.L. BULLOCK

LMBPN Publishing
PMB 196, 2540 South Maryland Pkwy
Las Vegas, NV 89109

First US Edition June, 2020
eBook ISBN: 978-1-64202-998-7
Print ISBN: 978-1-64202-999-4

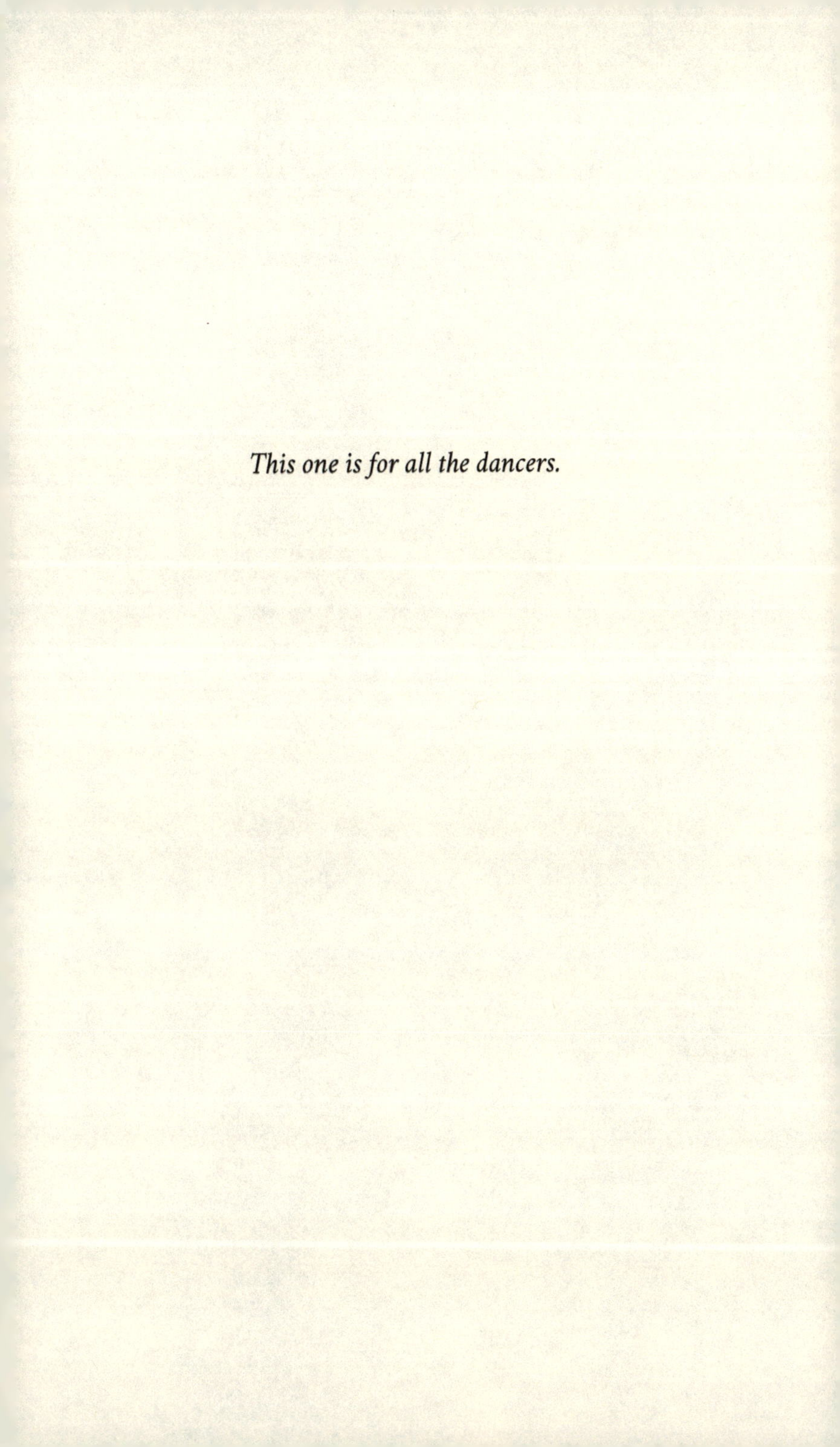

This one is for all the dancers.

THE DEAD AT MIDNIGHT TEAM

Thanks to our Beta Team:
John Ashmore, Kelly O'Donnell, Rachel Beckford, Mary
Morris

Thanks to the JIT Readers

Micky Cocker
Diane L. Smith
Jeff Goode
Angel LaVey
Veronica Stephan-Miller

If I've missed anyone, please let me know!

Editor
Lynne Stiegler

CHLOE

"There are major flaws in your plan, Lynn. Not just one or two. Have you actually thought this idea through? I mean, Joey? He's gay. I think I told you that." Walking down the stairs with my best friend, I shook my head, scarcely able to believe what I was hearing. I tossed her overnight bag up on my shoulder, grateful to have rekindled my relationship with Lynn. I hoped she felt the same about me, but what she was proposing was absolutely ridiculous. Talk about living in a fantasy world.

"I don't think being dead should mean he can't ever have love, Chloe. That's very shortsighted of you."

I snorted at her answer. "No, you're the one being shortsighted. He doesn't want your kind of love, Lynn."

"I've read that the paranormal world doesn't work the same way this one does. There are no limits there. It's more like soul love, not about gender or age or any of those temporal measurements. I'm not saying we're going to fall in love or anything, but Joey was kind of beautiful, wasn't he?"

"You just said those kinds of things don't matter. Which way are you going?"

She winked at me playfully. "I'm exploring all the possibilities. Are you sure Joey hasn't said anything about me? Nothing at all?"

"I think I would remember. No, he hasn't mentioned you in that way, Lynn. Sorry. Can we please change the subject? What happened to TJ? I thought you were crushing on him, girlfriend."

Lynn's expression shifted to what I called "stink face." She puckered her lips and flared her nose like she smelled something bad. "Yuck. He's not my type. Besides, it's not like Joey and I can ever actually hookup. Unless? Do ghosts…" She glanced up at me as we cleared the stairs. I was glad she was going home. Where had she come up with this idea? Too many sappy Hallmark movies, I guessed.

The sad thing was Lynn didn't realize Joey was walking behind us, sticking his finger down his throat to show me he was gagging over the idea. I ignored him and kept my eyes trained on Lynn. She only knew about Joey because he'd manifested himself at the Halloween party. After that, I felt pretty comfortable talking about him. Joey hadn't appeared to want to keep his existence a secret. I wondered if that had been a mistake.

This is your fault, Joey Agnes.

Stop calling me that. Can I help it if I'm fabulous?

At first, I'd thought Lynn was joking about her infatuation with Joey, but from this conversation, I could see I was dead wrong. My best friend *was* crushing on Joey. Awkward!

"Okay, Lynn. I'm not shortsighted, nor am I the kind of person who looks down on anyone because of their differences. I think being dead is a major impediment for any relationship, but what I was referring to was Joey's sexuality. He's gay, Lynn. He was gay when he was alive, and he is still gay. Sweet and a pain in the ass at times, but completely and totally gay." I saw Lynn's eyes moisten and her bottom lip tremble. I could almost predict what she was going to say next. I didn't have to be psychic to hear her thoughts.

I can change him...I'll be different. He will love me for me.

Better stop this conversation now. "Listen, girl. We stayed up pretty late last night, and you didn't get a lot of sleep. Neither did I. Please tell me it's the exhaustion talking. I know life's been hell at your house, but fantasizing about Joey is not the answer. You're talking crazy, Lynn. Keep it together. I'm going to talk to Aunt Tamara about you moving in, but you and Joey cannot happen. I need you to chill out!"

"Chill out about what?" Tamara walked into the foyer, her oversized glasses perched on her nose. She had her head buried in a stack of papers—no doubt the latest rendition of her book manuscript. Tamara was wrecking the ecosystem with her constant printer use. She'd been burning the midnight oil working on her new book while Lynn and I cruised the internet looking at tattoos and watching Hallmark movies. I had worked with Lynn to improve her energy too. The black aura, the one that emanated from her at the family home, was like sticky molasses. I could understand where it came from, her father, but it was affecting Lynn. It was an intensely negative aura, like a throbbing sickness. It would contaminate people who spent time near it if it was allowed to linger. The negativity had seeped into the walls and was now deeply embedded in her home—another reason to help her move out of that place.

I was proud of Tamara, but I missed hanging out with her sometimes. Between her new romance with the cop, her ghost stories, and Joey's incessant neediness, I rarely saw her anymore. Before I could answer Tamara in any kind of reasonably dishonest way, Lynn offered up her lie. "Tattoos. We're thinking about tattoos. Or at least I am. Chloe thinks I should wait, but I really want one. Kind of like a sleeve. Maybe some sort of fingerless glove with thorns, or a sugar skull with flames behind it. I'm not sure."

Tamara removed her glasses and trained her pretty eyes on Lynn. "Tattoos are wonderful personal expressions, but here's a tip I wish someone would have shared with me. Get tattoos only when you're feeling good about life. Tattoos that memorialize painful memories aren't easily erased." She smiled and slid her glasses back on her face.

I snorted in surprise. "Don't tell us you have some guy's name tattooed on your behind."

She scowled at the suggestion. "Even I knew not to do that. I will say this, though: avoid putting tattoos in any personal areas. Doing so can lead to some embarrassing conversations later. Just saying."

"Tamara!"

Lynn laughed at Tamara's confession, and I opened the front door. "Thanks for the tip. Later, y'all!" Lynn said. I handed Lynn her bag, and she hurried to get home before her dad returned from his latest road trip. Lynn had said things were not getting better there, but she was getting better at not being there. Between working at the ice cream shop with me and trying to finish school, she stayed pretty busy. At least on that front, things were better for her. I closed the door and breathed a sigh of relief, as did Joey, who was leaning against the door beside me.

Tamara watched us curiously. "What's going on with you two? Did I miss something?"

Joey peeked out the blinds to make sure Lynn's car was actually exiting the property. "You have no idea how exhausting she is, Chloe. Constantly trying to summon me. I mean, it doesn't even work like that. You need to vote her off the island and don't even think about bringing her here permanently. She's a mixed bag of nuts, that one."

Tamara searched for answers as I began trying to explain the reason for Joey's histrionics without showing my hand. This wasn't how I wanted to have this conversation. "What do you mean permanently? She's been summoning you?"

Joey posed awkwardly and peeked through the blinds again. "Try to catch up, Tamara! How could Lynn think I would be interested in her? I'm dead! Sorry. I don't mean to be ugly. I heard you try to lay the truth down, but Lynn's not processing any of it. I'd be more interested in the lawn guy than her. Let's just be honest; Roland is not my type. Ugh. I'm going to my room. Handle it, Chloe. I don't want her mooning over me all the time."

Joey began walking or trying to walk up the stairs. Once again, from the knees down, he was pretty transparent. When he got to the top landing, he looked over his shoulder and said, "Told you I was a heartbreaker. Later!" A few seconds later, we heard his bedroom door slam. It was an entirely ridiculous situation, but what could we do but laugh?

He was right, of course. Lynn was misdirecting her emotions, but according to the marathon of Hallmark movies we'd watched, she wouldn't be the first girl to fall for a ghost. Joey's hasty departure left me trying to explain to Tamara what was up with Lynn. She agreed with me. Lynn's crushing on Joey was merely an expression of her desire to escape her current situation.

As I walked with Tamara to her office, I considered talking to her about inviting Lynn to stay. Lynn had asked if she could move in, but honestly, I wasn't sure how *I* felt about that. I liked Lynn a lot and enjoyed her company, but only in small doses. If Lynn was going to engage in this kind of craziness with Joey, I wasn't sure this was the place for her. The family home, commonly referred to as the Dead House, had more than its share of spiritual activity. We didn't need anyone here summoning the dead. Even I had no idea she was trying to do that.

Lately, we had been in something of a spiritual lull, but it wouldn't stay that way. As sure as my name was Chloe Carol, I knew that for a fact. Small things still happened from time to time, like my change purse or hairbrush would disappear. I would find them in weird places, too. Once, I found the word *cursed* written all over my notebook cover in red ink. At least I think it was ink. I couldn't be sure.

"What's on your mind? Did you girls stay up too late last night?" I pretended Tamara wasn't treating me like a kid. She did that sometimes. However, I knew she was doing the best she could, and so far, she'd managed to keep us all safe. And most of us were alive. "You look like you have something on your mind, Chloe. You may as well tell me what it is."

The house popped around us. The Ridaught Plantation was so old it made noises whenever the weather threatened to change. Let the temperatures drop or have a storm roll through, and the place sounded like someone was stomping around on packing peanuts. The Dead House was like a paranormal thermometer.

Today, every plank and every piece of trim creaked. Did Tamara notice? Our home felt very unsettled. Not just because of Lynn's weirdness or Tamara's hyper-focus on her paranormal work, or even the fact that Joey roamed the halls without legs. It was the curse springing to life.

I'm cursed. Isn't that nice? Not just me, but all the women in our family. It all began with Lavinia Loper. A sudden chill made the hair on my arms rise dramatically. I didn't want to talk out loud about the curse in the house. This place had eyes and ears. Maybe later, if we went into town to grab some pizza as was our usual weekend custom, I'd open this line of conversation. Last I heard the curse breaker, a woman named Angela Webster, was driving over from Mobile, but there was some sort of delay in her schedule.

The sooner, the better.

When I'd done some preliminary study of my immediate family tree, I was shocked. I discovered most of the women in my mother's family line died at a young age. Rarely did they live past forty, with the exception of my grandmother Louise. How she ever accomplished that I had no idea. She was dead, so I couldn't pick her brain, and she wasn't the kind of woman who would appreciate being contacted after death. She had never been a friendly woman, but she did provide me with a home when my mother had gone on her tours, which had been quite often. Louise was not the loving grandmotherly sort of woman you hoped to have as a grandparent.

As if Tamara read my mind, she said, "Let's head to town and grab some pizza if you're in the mood." That was our code phrase for, "Hey, let's talk outside of the house." I was glad I didn't have to explain. "We can go now if you're in the mood and aren't doing anything. I need to stop a few other places, actually. You down for that?"

"Sounds great, Aunt Tamara. I just need to put some shoes on. Meet you back here in a few minutes." I hugged her and I could tell she hadn't expected it. What had gotten into me lately, being all lovey-dovey with Tamara and Joey? Some people would call it personal growth. Whatever it was, it felt good.

Joey met me in the hallway, and naturally he'd been eavesdropping. I reminded him that a dramatic entrance only worked if you left the scene. It was rude to listen in on private conversations.

"I'm out for a while. Stay out of trouble and my makeup."

To my surprise, he didn't beg me to stay. Instead, he presented me with a list of things he wanted me to pick up for him. I accepted the dirty piece of paper as I carefully avoided touching his cold hand. He had a towel wrapped around his head for some reason. Clearly, he was trying to do something with his eyebrows because they looked all out of whack. He was still a bit lackluster in color, but if he felt good enough to pluck his eyebrows, I guessed he was doing okay.

God knew what was going on in that room of his. He rarely let me in, which was highly suspicious. Before he had a room, he spent all his time in mine. Then I heard a man's voice.

"Who's in there?" I blurted out. "Do you have company?" He never had visitors unless you counted his ghost cat, which he sometimes called Mr. Ruffles or Pinkerton. I wondered if he actually remembered what he'd named the animal. That was definitely no cat I heard in there now.

"Joey, does Tamara know you have guys over?"

"Can't a guy have any privacy in this place? If you see my cat, let me know. And for the record, his name is Mr. Pinkerton. You have my list. Later." He vanished into his bedroom door, which simultaneously closed in my face. Instinctively, I knocked on it, which didn't do me a bit of good. Joey had his radio going, and the air had an electric vibe that unsettled me. Too much collected energy made me sick, and the place was throbbing with it. I gave his list a cautious glance.

Hell no, I wasn't going to buy him razors. And what was that? So ridiculous. Was everyone in this house dating except me?

This list had Tamara's name written all over it. Just wait until Tamara got a load of this. I shoved Joey's list in my pocket and went in search of my purse. I hurried into my room to grab it and my shoes.

My purse wasn't where it had just been. As Tamara called me from downstairs, I began digging for it.

2

CHLOE

Joey? You better not be pulling a prank on me.

I'm busy, sunshine. What prank?

I hadn't made my bed that morning, so there was a possibility my purse was hidden under the jumbled-up comforter. I snatched it off the bed, but my efforts yielded nothing. I got on my knees to search under the bed.

My purse is missing again. I'm pretty sure Tamara didn't take it. Joey?

No time for this chit chat. Wasn't me. Later, tater.

My slouchy purse wasn't very large, and it could have fallen off while Lynn and I were chatting. Joey wasn't great at lying. If he'd been tinkering around with it, I was pretty sure I would have known. He had no qualms about invading my personal space, but he wasn't a liar.

Evasive. Yes.

A good liar? No.

I moved a few things around beneath the bed to get a good look. I had some storage boxes under there stuffed with photos and postcards I'd found in Mom's trunks.

After shifting the items around, I spotted the vintage denim pouch.

How in the world did it get here stuffed behind the boxes? That was just weird. If Joey didn't do it, and Lynn didn't, someone else had. My room's energy barrier was down, and apparently, anyone could walk in.

As I reached for my purse, an odd sound caught my attention.

Tick. Tick. Tick.

The sound I heard was the steady ticking of a clock. My digital clock did not make those kinds of sounds. I had a watch, but it was also digital, and there were no other clockworks or any reason for there to be ticking.

I slid under my bed and was moving boxes around when I caught an odd pattern in the wood. The flooring was off—slightly raised and uneven. I could feel it. The whole section of flooring appeared smooth, but the one patch appeared older and rougher. I rubbed my hand over it to confirm. It was different. I didn't normally get focused on things like this, but I had to take a closer look.

Joey? Why is there a ticking sound coming from my floor?

No answer. Not a peep. Tamara called me from downstairs, but I couldn't turn away from my current task. She would just have to wait a minute.

My bed wasn't heavy, not a sleigh bed like Lynn's. Nothing fancy, it had a simple antique frame with a metal headboard with ceramic floral details. As I slid out from under the bed, I shoved the comforter out of the way and tossed the purse on the mattress as I nudged the furniture from the spot I wanted to investigate.

Finally, I could see the floor good and proper. I

squatted next to it and rubbed my fingers over the obvious edges of a strange cut-out. The bit of wood was definitely off, and different. It was a hiding spot I realized. I knelt, and with some hesitation, put my ear next to the floor.

Tick. Tick.

I could hear it, the ticking. Tick. Tick. It had to be a clock. What else made a ticking sound? A bomb? That was ridiculous. Who would put a bomb in the floor of my room? The only way to know what I was looking at would be to open this puppy up. I examined the wood and could find no visible screw marks or nails. Hm…no tools needed then. I used my fingernails on the edges of one board and, after a few painful attempts, successfully lifted it up. A few more tries and I got a good finger hold beneath it. The board came up. The second was even easier.

It was a hiding spot!

The hole was dark and shallow, but the ticking grew louder.

There was nothing to do but investigate. I should probably have used my flashlight or the app on my phone, but I was transfixed by the hidden treasure that had been beneath my floor. I wondered how long it had been there. I've been living in this house for almost six months, and I had never heard ticking before. Why was this clock ticking now?

"Chloe? What are you doing?" I heard Tamara's worried voice behind me, but I couldn't answer her. My shaking hands reached into the darkness.

3

ANNABEL

"Do you hear the clock, Annabel? Don't you lie to me, don't you dare lie to me. You got to tell the truth. You're too old to be telling a bald-faced lie to old Anita. You be a grown girl, my Annabel. You hear the clock, don't you?" Anita's dark face hovered before me. Her chilly hands rubbed mine lovingly. I hated seeing the desperation in her old face. As always, I wanted to make things right, to please everyone, but I could not lie about this.

I lied quite often, and the older I got, the easier I spun my tales. It was always easier to tell a lie. People liked to hear what they wanted to hear. Lying allayed spankings. Lies put smiles on faces. Lying would send me to hell, but life, at least my life, was made better by it.

"No, Poppa. I never touched your pipe."

"No, Miss Haynes. I don't know what happened to your matches."

"No, Anita. I didn't take the letter. I didn't see a letter at all."

Lies associated with my love of fire were more difficult to offer successfully. I had to be very careful with those lies. I had to be extra careful when stealing things like matches or tobacco and not to make my fires close to the house too.

Despite her piercing stare and gentle hands, I wasn't sure about making a confession.

"Tell me the truth, Annabel. Don't you lie to me." Anita continued to rub my hands lovingly. My heart beat fast in my chest. The wild, angry face of the clock was on the mantelpiece. Anita was hunkered down in her favorite chair. I never liked the clock even though it was one of my mother's most treasured possessions. Up until recently, I'd never heard the clock make a sound. Now I heard it night and day.

Once in a while, the ugly clock played awful music, but never when I expected it. Never on the hour or half-hour, and one could never read time by it. The clock was always wrong, despite the carefully painted gold numerals that occasionally shimmered with an unearthly glow. I was not very old and, according to my governess, not very smart, but even I comprehended this was not a normal device. The downstairs clock played lovely chimes twice an hour. It was always predictable and always soothing. This clock offered no such peaceful sounds.

"Yes, ma'am. I hear it." Anita's deep brown eyes watered as she released my hands.

"I knew you would hear it. One day, I knew you would hear it. Just like she did. I hoped to God. I prayed you would never hear it, but I can see the curse is doing its work. I should never have agreed to contain it, but she would not be moved, Annabel. I tried to capture it, but it was beyond my power. It's not my fault, dear child. Don't you hate old Anita."

My mouth suddenly felt dry and sour at the same time. "I could never hate you. What curse, Anita?" My voice dropped to a whisper. "Am I cursed? Was Momma cursed?"

Anita patted her eyes with a gray handkerchief. After a minute, she covered her mouth with the damp fabric. She sobbed into it but offered me neither a denial nor a confirmation. I put my arms around her neck and hugged her while I pondered whether or not I should have lied.

Yes, I probably should have lied, but it was harder to lie to Anita than anyone else.

"We are going to try something. We are going to try and break this curse, little Annabel. We're going to try."

"When? How, Anita? I don't understand."

She hugged me tight and patted my back before releasing me. "We have to hide the clock. I need some time. That's what we'll do. We will hide it, Annie, and you will never hear it again, okay? I'll try again. Don't you look for it, don't you talk to it, don't do nothing about it. Promise me? No, you better swear to me!"

She pointed her stubby finger at me, and I nodded obediently. I watched in silence as Anita took the clock and ordered me to sit in the chair and watch the fire. I did as she asked. I added wood when the fire got low. I poked it with the metal stick and squatted before it.

I could see everything in the fire. I loved the flames and wished I could live in them. I would be at home in the warmth and the flickering colors. As I stared, I felt sleepy and trancelike.

I could see Anita and the clock.

I wasn't trying to see her. I wasn't trying to spy on her, but I knew exactly where she hid the clock.

I knew one day I would have to go look for it, but for now, I stared into the flames and lost my way in the fire, as I always did. It was easy to do. Sometimes I could see Momma's face staring back at me, and sometimes I saw the other woman's face, the one who looked like Momma. There were others. My family, all women with eyes like mine, their eyes wide with fear, and their mouths opened in silent screams.

Then I saw the girl.

4

TAMARA

Chloe's room was never an orderly place, but she was sitting on the floor and staring into a hole. Her bed had been moved, and the teen wasn't moving. It was as if she were frozen in time, her pale hand above the space before her. Seeing Chloe's hand reaching into that hole filled me with dread.

"Wait! Chloe, wait!"

Naturally, as always with Chloe, she didn't pay attention to my warning. Her hands plunged through the spider webs and disappeared into the darkness. As she sat back, I hovered over her as she revealed a shiny black clock. It was an ugly item that didn't go with this house at all. The clock was old, very old and it was like nothing I had ever seen with its black lacquer paint. It had a gold dial and numerals on the clock face, which was covered with dirty glass.

Something about it was terrifying. Chloe held it up to me, but I didn't want to touch it. The round clock part was a screaming mouth, and over it was a slanted, flared nose. Above the screaming mouth and nose were two fierce eyes.

They were precise and appeared more like fine wood carving than a lacquered object.

"Geesh, Chloe." The clock was an actual face, and it wasn't pretty to look at. It was gross and interesting at the same time. "What in God's name did you find?"

Chloe tried to hand it to me again, but I encouraged her to put it on the floor. I did not want to touch it, which seemed silly as I'd handled worse things in the past. The Elizabeth doll from the Clayton Hotel sprang to mind. I didn't have a good feeling about this clock. I dug my phone out of my purse and took a picture of it accidentally while trying to access my flashlight app.

"Thanks, Tamara. Now I'm blind. Hey, there's something else in here." Shining the light in the hole, we saw a small grimy looking book and a little tin like an antique candy box. Chloe reached in and grabbed them, then put them on the floor beside the clock. My hand reached for the book, but I withdrew it.

"How did you find these things? They must be covered with a hundred years of dirt, despite being in that hole."

Chloe stared at the items between us as I squatted on the floor next to her. "I went looking for my purse and heard the clock ticking. I moved a few things around, and here we are. I never knew this spot was in the floor. Did you?"

"It's not ticking," I said as I tucked my hair behind my ear and tilted my head toward the clock.

"What are you talking about? It's ticking so loud I can barely hear you." She rubbed her dusty hands on her jeans and shrugged as she stared at me questioningly. "I would never have found it if not for the ticking. Wait, it stopped. I can hear you fine now. What is this thing?"

I twisted my lips as I pondered her question. We needed to chat, but not here. As they say, these walls had ears. "Let's put all this in a box and take it downstairs. We can check it out when we get back. I'm ready for pizza, what about you?" I touched her arm and nodded my head to remind her to agree with me.

"Oh, yeah. I'm starving. Let me see if I have a box in my closet." The idea of either of us handling these items too much unsettled me. Whoever placed these things in the floor cubby had done so a long time ago.

We needed to get out of here.

Chloe scrounged around in her closet and found an old gift bag. We quickly put everything in the bag and took it downstairs. It was quiet in Joey's room at the moment. I could've sworn I heard music playing in there earlier, but I wasn't one to look a gift horse in the mouth. He'd been on his best behavior lately, much to my relief. Giving him his own room had been a great idea, after all.

We deposited the gift bag on the foyer table and exited the Ridaught Plantation with quiet determination. We weren't running away from danger, just playing it safe in case there was more happening than met the eye. There usually was around here. We'd barely gotten out of the driveway when Chloe began talking a hundred miles an hour.

"You have to be joking! I heard that clock ticking, and I've never heard ticking before in that room. Why would an old clock start ticking and then quit?"

I adjusted the mirror as I wheeled on to the highway.

Chloe always tinkered with my mirrors when she used the car.

"I can't understand why you couldn't hear that loud, obnoxious ticking. There was something else. As I was reaching into the hole, I saw something, a moment in time. I saw Annabel and Anita. They were talking about the clock…shoot!"

"What is it, Chloe?"

She closed her eyes and held her hands up as if she were trying to access some sort of invisible panel. Mediums are weird. "I can't remember it all. It's like the more I try, the more I forget."

"Tell me what you do remember before you forget. Spill it!" Chloe did as I asked, but the memory was fragmented. The last thing she remembered was Anita crying over the clock. I didn't know what to say except to encourage her to be patient and let the spirit world do its work. Obviously, the clock wanted Chloe to find it, but why? *I probably should've said something to Joey. He'd be the first one to go play with it.*

As if to confirm my fears, the phone began to ring. It wasn't like Joey could call me. He hadn't been able to master making phone calls yet, though he'd burned up two of my phones trying.

"Will you see who's calling, please? Wait, that's not my ringtone."

I was hoping Angela Webster would call me back today, but so far, I'd heard nothing. I guess curse breakers were in high demand.

She dug in her purse and produced her purple, sequin-covered phone. "It's not mine. Mine's right here." Chloe immediately began ransacking my bag and pulled out mine. It was definitely my phone ringing, but I would never have selected the ringtone. It wasn't a tone, per se, more like an old-fashioned song played by a maniacal harpsichordist. As Chloe tapped on the screen to answer the call, the car began to shudder and it quickly died. "Oh, crap!" I shouted as I tugged at the dead wheel and managed to navigate safely off the road.

"Are we out of gas? Is the oil light on?"

"No, I don't think so." I tapped on the oil and gas gauges, but everything looked okay. "Has it been acting up?" Chloe often drove my car to work, but we hadn't had any issues with it. Except for changing my radio stations and shifting my mirrors. That I could live with.

"It's been running like a champ for me. Oh no! Is that smoke coming out of the engine?"

We both got out, and I was mortified to see my car was on fire. I uttered a string of profanities as I raced back and grabbed our purses and my cell phone. I also managed to commandeer the keys before the smoke began to boil out from under the hood.

"What is wrong with the car?" I screamed.

Chloe shouted back, "I don't know!"

I called 911, and they promised to send someone out quickly. True to their word, it only took minutes for them to arrive, but by the time they pulled up, my car was shot, completely ablaze. Chloe and I watched in shock. *What the hell just happened?*

The fire truck began hosing the thing down, but it was too little too late. The air smelled like burnt rubber, and I began choking as the firefighters pushed us to the other side of the road. Kevin pulled up in his patrol vehicle. Chloe and I went to meet him.

"Y'all okay?" he asked with genuine concern. "It just started smoking? Did you hear an explosion?"

"No. Nothing at all. It died, and then it caught on fire. I didn't hear a ping or anything that would indicate there was something wrong. One minute we were driving down the road, and the next minute, the car stalled, then it burst into flames. We were lucky it didn't catch on fire while we were still inside. Has there been a recall I don't know about?"

"Anything is possible." Kevin patted my shoulder in an attempt to comfort me. I didn't refuse his attempt. "Stay by my car, and I'll go over to talk to the trooper. Is there anything valuable in there?"

I shook my head. "Just Chloe and me, and we have our purses. I wouldn't ask the firefighters to risk their lives to retrieve paperwork."

"Okay. I'll be back."

Chloe and I leaned up against his vehicle, both of us shaking our heads at the sight of the family car melting before our eyes. "Are you going to tell me you don't think the phone call is related?" I couldn't account for the weird ringtone, neither could I be sure that our car problems weren't directly related, but that clock…

Chloe didn't say a word, but she was probably thinking the same thing. This was a total nightmare. Kevin came back in about five minutes to give us the expected report. The car was a total loss. Damn. I knew that. It had been on fire. It wasn't a new vehicle, and I had good insurance, so replacing it wasn't a problem.

"I'll take you guys home. The fire department is going hook her up, and they'll take it to the tow yard once it's cooled down. They'll have to wait a while. So, no problems with the vehicle before this?"

I slung my sagging purse up on my shoulder. "Not a problem at all. I'll just have to get a rental until the insurance company replaces it. Would you mind taking us home, Kevin?"

Chloe interrupted and shook her head vigorously. "No. I don't want to go home. Not yet. I don't mean to sound like a brat, but I just can't go back there. Please, Tamara. If you could drop us off at the pizza place, Kevin, I'm sure I could get Lynn to take us home." Chloe wiped her eyes with the back of her hand. I glanced at Kevin, who, by his expression, had every intention of doing as she asked.

"Big Brother's Pizza okay?"

She smiled, and we climbed into his car to wait for Kevin while he spoke to the trooper. Kevin returned with a confident expression. He was doing his best to pretend everything was normal, but all three of us knew better.

There was nothing normal about any of this.

5

TAMARA

Kevin kept his eyes on the road, but he did glance at me briefly. "What's really going on?" I studied his side profile. Was he trying to grow a beard? His five o'clock shadow looked especially dark this afternoon.

"What makes you ask?"

"Come on. I'm not a rookie when it comes to that house and the people who live there."

I caught a glimpse of Chloe in the side mirror. She'd leaned back in the seat and was staring out the window. "Chloe found a weird clock under her bed. It was hidden in the floorboards. She said it was ticking. I didn't hear a thing, but as you know, Chloe is a medium so it's entirely possible only she could hear it."

"Tell him about the ringtone." Chloe watched me from the deputy's side mirror. I did, and he didn't know what to say. Neither did I. Kevin answered a call, and we uncomfortably eavesdropped as he pulled into the parking lot, but he wasn't in a hurry to get out.

"What about the lady from Mobile? The lady who works with curses."

"I spoke to her, but she had some scheduling issues and was supposed to call me back. I'm still waiting, but she's not the only curse breaker on the planet." A flashing light came on the front of the pizza shop, an indicator that fresh pizza was hot and ready. I wasn't hungry in the slightest, but Chloe needed normalcy. I wouldn't deny her that.

"Just think, my grandmother and maybe Mom knew all about the family curse, but never told me a thing. I find that incredible unless Mom didn't know about it. Louise knew everything about everyone. She must have known. It has to be my ancestor Annabel. The one I saw in the vision."

Kevin removed the keys and turned slightly to meet her gaze. "Vision?"

"I don't want to talk about it. All I know is things are going to get worse, you guys. Don't ask me how I know, but I do, just as sure as I know my name is Chloe Carol. I found that clock for a reason."

"We'll figure it out together, Chloe," I replied as I got out of the car. My clothes smelled like burned rubber. "Let's go get pizza. I'd like to think about something besides ghosts and curses and flaming cars."

We went inside and luckily, there weren't many other customers hanging around. We had the buffet to ourselves, which suited me just fine. I needed normal, too. The Ridaught Plantation was a paranormal playground, but I'd left that scene, or so I thought. Kevin paid for our meals even though I asked him not to and we hunkered down in a corner booth. Chloe and Kevin had piled their plates high, but after dousing my slice with Parmesan cheese, I realized I couldn't even pretend to have an appetite.

I could say the same thing about Chloe, who was pulling the pepperoni off her slices and not eating the actual pizza.

What a day. We'd left the house expecting to spend a happy afternoon together and instead witnessed the death of our beloved car. Now we were having pizza with a cop and the conversation we were supposed to have didn't look like it was going to happen.

"What's up with Lynn?" I sipped my soda as I waited for Chloe to fill me in on her friend's strange behavior. Kevin stuffed his face, but he was listening to every word.

Chloe wiped her mouth with a napkin and said in a whisper, "Lynn's father is an abuser, Aunt Tamara. It's not a secret." She directed that last comment to Kevin, who was keeping quiet and eating. "Her father abuses her physically and certainly verbally. She doesn't have anywhere to go, not since Trey left to work with his dad."

Kevin paused his feasting and added, "I hadn't heard that. That's a shame. I was hoping that kid could make a break from his father. He always seemed like he had a good head on his shoulders. Unfortunately for Trey and Lynn, their fathers are very much like their grandfather. He wasn't a nice guy either. I can't talk about open cases, but I can assure you I've heard this before. Lynn is over seventeen now, right?"

"Yes, that's right. What does that mean?" Chloe answered hopefully. I knew where this conversation was going. "She can't leave without somewhere to go, Aunt Tamara. She doesn't have anywhere else, just us. Lynn is a good person, despite her infatuation with Joey. She needs a place to crash, so she can finish school, and you know she has a job, so I was thinking…"

"Chloe? What about the curse? We can't bring Lynn into a situation where she might get hurt. I understand what you're saying. I don't want her to get hurt, but do you think being at our place while we're trying to figure this out is the best idea?"

"She's there almost all the time now. Spending a few more nights a week isn't going to make a difference, Tamara."

I noticed I'd lost the "aunt" moniker, but she had a point. Before I could offer a counterpoint, Chloe tossed her napkin on the table and mumbled something unpleasant as she left for the bathroom. I shrugged my shoulders in frustration. "Do you think I'm crazy? I mean, I have a point, right?"

"Yes, but so does she, Tamara. Look, I'm not getting in the middle of what you guys have going on, but I encourage you to think about it before you say no. Of the two brothers, Buck and Jack, Jack is the more volatile and a mean alcoholic. If you do decide to allow Lynn to stay, promise me you will make it official. Lynn would need to get a protection order. That way, if he shows up at the Ridaught place, you'll have every right to have him arrested. There's no better place for Jack to be than in jail. Like I said, just think about it."

I leaned on my folded hands and pondered his advice. "I didn't expect to make any major decisions today. My car burned to cinders, and now my teenager wants to bring in another teenager. I'll be honest, I'm not really sure how I feel about Lynn. Just this morning, she was talking about getting a fingerless glove tattoo." I moved my pizza around.

"What do you have against tattoos? I know for a fact you have one or two yourself." He grinned, which was a little less appealing than it would've normally been with pizza sauce on the corner of his mouth. I offered him a napkin.

"I have nothing against Lynn, but she's just reckless. I get that vibe from her, and believe me, I know that vibe. I don't know, Kevin. Here comes Chloe. Change of subject, please."

He shoved his plate to the side and wiped his hands with yet another napkin. "I do have a case for you two if you're interested. A cold case." He leaned forward and dropped his voice to a whisper. "The victim's name is Rachel Burns, young, pretty, and violently murdered. By the way, Sheriff Jarvis would really like to meet you. I haven't told him you are a paranormal investigator, just a researcher, so please play along."

My cheeks flamed a little. What was he saying? He didn't want to be embarrassed by me, or he didn't want others to know he believed? I let it go but stored that nugget in the back of my mind. Eventually, we would have to talk about my disapproval of being his dirty little secret.

Chloe appeared very interested in the prospect of participating in his investigation. "Rachel Burns? Why does her name sound so familiar to me? I know I've heard that name before."

"Rachel Burns was Crystal Springs' one and only movie star. She was pretty popular, here in her hometown and in Hollywood. Rachel was murdered during a vacation back home in 2005. Her parents' property line, butts up against yours on the western side. Remarkably enough, the place is vacant. Occasionally I get a call to go out there because people see lights. I've found evidence of candles and fires being burnt in the fireplace. No offense, but sometimes teenagers like to go scare themselves."

"Oh, that's right! The Burns' house. Rachel Burns, she was the girl in that horror flick. *Butterfly Web*, right?" Chloe leaned forward, completely mesmerized by this turn of conversation. "No joke, but yeah, the teenagers around here are obsessed with that place. Almost as much as ours."

"If you send me what you can, I'll take a look at it, Kevin. I am in the middle of a book, and we have this other situation to take care of, so I can't promise anything," I commented. I took another sip of my drink. It was the middle of the day, but I sure wished I had ordered beer instead. I could use a good beer right about now. My head was whirling.

"I'd be happy to take a look," Chloe offered without even looking at me. "I don't have much going on except for work. I've done all my homework. After these finals are over, that's it for me. Senior year is done."

"Tamara?" Kevin prompted me as if he were asking me permission. Maybe he was.

"Go for it, Chloe. I'll help too. If you don't mind, I'd like to go home now. I need to call the insurance company and figure out what I'm going to do with my car." We wrapped up our half-eaten lunch and headed home, pausing briefly to observe the scorch marks on the side of the road. Evidence of my car's fiery demise. The three of us didn't talk much the rest of the drive home. What was there to say?

"Can I come by later? I get off at six. I can bring the cold case info for Chloe, and maybe we can chill out," Kevin said from his open car window.

"Let's play it by ear, okay? I'm not a hundred percent on board with asking her to get involved in yet another murder case. You should have said something to me privately before inviting her to help you."

I pretended not to notice his disappointment, but I knew I was right about this. I had a responsibility to keep Chloe safe. At least, as safe as possible. Chloe disappeared into the house ahead of me, and I watched Kevin's car wind down the driveway.

I was kind of sad to see him go. I liked having him around.

No time for deep thoughts about life and love, Tamara. You've got to have a serious conversation with Joey about uninvited guests and ponder the wisdom of basically adopting yet another teenager. I could barely manage Chloe, much less Lynn. Not to mention a phone call to the car insurance people. I felt overwhelmed.

Chloe's muffled scream inside the house shook me out of my emotional doldrums. I raced inside.

6

TAMARA

I entered the house and immediately ran to Chloe. She was on the floor opposite the table, and it appeared as if she'd been flung there. I thought I caught the tail end of someone whizzing around the corner, but I couldn't be sure who it was. It didn't look like Joey's skinny behind.

"Chloe!" Her stunned expression worried me. Her arms were flung above her head and she was sliding to the floor, her eyelids batting as if she were going to pass out. I heard her moan as I scurried toward her. A black shadow moved oddly, like a blob of molasses, across the floor from the foyer to the living room. Chloe's eyes were closing as her body sagged. I didn't see blood or bruises, but I was no nurse. "Joey! Where are you?" There was no answer from my ghostly BFF as I dug in my purse for my phone. I had every intention of calling 911 when Chloe moaned a swearword I'd never heard her use before.

She suddenly came awake and swung at me as if she had no idea what had just happened. "Hey! It's me. It's me,

Tamara." I hung up the phone, and it clattered on the floor. "Talk to me!"

Chloe swore again and tried to sit up. "I don't know what it was, but it hit me. Oh, my head! Is there a bruise on this side? A shadow charged me, and it surprised me. I couldn't tell if it was a man or a woman. Did you see it?"

"A blob of blackness, that's what I saw. You might need to get your head examined—at the hospital, I mean." Chloe thought that was funny. She started laughing and, to my surprise, couldn't stop. Forget that a black shadow knocked her for a loop, she was guffawing like a crazy person.

She finally said, "I probably do need my head examined, but not today. I don't need a doctor or a hospital. Oh no! The clock, the book and the tin—they're gone. I guess whatever that was took them! Have you seen Joey?" Chloe was trying to get on her feet, but not having a good go of it. I glanced over to the table where we'd left the clock and she was absolutely correct. *Joey?*

"Let's get you into the living room. No arguments, Chloe. You need to chill for a few minutes." As I helped Chloe get back on her feet and into the living room, I kept my eye on the hallway. If there was something here strong enough to shove someone to the ground and steal things, then we might not be out of danger. "Can you stay here a minute while I go upstairs to see if Joey is okay? Or would you rather I wait with you?" I wasn't exactly sure what I needed to do. I basically had two teenagers to take care of, and I wanted to make sure they were both safe.

Chloe leaned back on the couch with her hand on her forehead. "I think I'm going to need some ice. I don't sense anything now. Whatever or whoever it was, I think it is gone."

"Good. I'll get you some ice." I scurried down the hall, keeping my eyes on the floor just in case the black shadow wanted to manifest and repeat its performance. I opened the freezer to grab the soft ice pack I kept for accidents like these. I couldn't have anticipated anyone would get smacked by a ghost, but when you do renovation work in an old house, someone was always going to need a Band-Aid or an ice pack. We'd been doing a lot of renovation work recently, and I wondered if maybe that had contributed to today's activity. Where was the ice pack? I knew I had seen it this morning.

"Tamara?" A familiar voice echoed in my ear.

"Joey! You scared the crap out of me! Where have you been? Hiding in the dryer? Something just attacked Chloe, and I need an ice pack. Is that the ice pack?" I put my hand on my hip suspiciously, and he hid it behind his back. "Come on. Hand it over." With a dramatic sigh, he handed the pack over, and I tossed it back in the freezer. I reached for a bag of frozen peas instead.

"Sorry. My eyes were a tad puffy. Who attacked Chloe? You said someone was in the house? Was it that Trey kid? I knew he was bad news." Joey's hand went to his chest, and his fingers fluttered as if he was trying to give himself additional air. He wasn't very luminous today, but he was no less himself when it came to the dramatics. I eyed him suspiciously, but clearly, he had no idea anyone else had been here.

"Wrong. It wasn't anyone living. A shadow just about knocked her out." He immediately yelped and headed out of the kitchen. I followed him to the living room. Chloe was texting on her phone. She wasn't going to die, but she had a noticeable bump on her forehead. "The ice pack wasn't available. Try these peas."

"Peas?"

I shrugged as I sat beside her. With a disgusted sigh, she slapped the bag to the side of her head and gave Joey a sideways glance. "Did you take the clock?"

"What clock?" Joey asked as he hovered beside her, his hands in his jean's pockets. He wore a faded blue t-shirt, and his hair hung in his eyes. He wasn't lying. Joey had no idea what we were talking about.

"Chloe found a clock in her room. It was hidden in the floor. We brought it downstairs, along with a few other things. When we came back, they were gone. Has anyone been in here? Anyone at all?"

"Nobody who would steal a clock. Do you think maybe you ran up on a ghost, it startled you, and you fell? That kind of thing happens to me all the time." Joey sat down beside Chloe, but he didn't get too close. I wasn't feeling great, Joey wasn't very luminous, and Chloe just got hit by something.

"No. I didn't trip and fall. I saw a shadow figure, and Tamara did too. Are you sure you don't know where the clock is? We have to find that clock and the book and that little box. I should never have left them." Chloe shifted the bag of frozen peas. "Man, that hurts." She sighed as we sat watching her. I didn't know what else to do. It wasn't like I could call Kevin and report an intruder.

Joey bit his bottom lip and crossed his invisible legs. He avoided making eye contact. "I have something to tell you both, but I want you to hear me out. It's not like I did this to hurt anyone, and I do not think it's related. I allowed Aaron to visit me, okay? He was just here for a few minutes. I mean, he is not very strong, and he's never coming back. It was a one-time deal. He's fully on the other side now. I forgave him, and that's that."

Chloe dropped her peas and gasped. To my surprise, she reached for Joey's hand. Usually, she avoided direct contact with the dead, but this was a special moment. I wanted to cry myself and forgot about the shadowy attacker. "Joey, I'm so proud of you. That is such a good thing to hear, and I needed to hear something good today. I hope you are okay. How do you feel?"

He sniffed and waned a little more. He'd faded so much he was unable to hold anyone's hand. "I'm not really sure. I am glad I never have to see him again. I'm glad he's gone for good." Joey's voice broke slightly, but he didn't vanish.

"Does that mean you're going to be leaving us? I don't want you to leave," Chloe asked, her voice sounding ragged and heartbroken.

His sad smile broke my heart. "I couldn't have him coming back forever. It wasn't right, no matter what he did to me. I have to go. Do you feel weird?" Joey flickered as he waved his hands in front of his face. "It's too hot in here. I'm going to have to go soon." Just like that, he was flickering like a candle.

Chloe perked up and dropped the peas on the coffee table. "I didn't want to say anything, but I haven't felt good since the car burst into flames. Tamara's car caught on fire, Joey. Then we came home, and something attacked me. I think it's the family curse acting up. Could Aaron have taken the clock with him?"

Joey closed his eyes for a moment and got very still. He hovered between the couch and the door. When he was feeling supernaturally healthy, he did us the courtesy of simulating breathing. He did a lot of things the living did just to make us feel comfortable. It took a lot of energy, but whatever he experienced today had drained him of all of that extraneous power.

"Not Aaron, Chloe. Oh, my head." His head did kind of wobble in his hands. "Root cellar. Backyard. It wasn't Aaron. He's not coming back, he got what he needed. I set him free. It's not him." Joey was fading quickly.

"Joey? Don't leave. Don't leave for good. Promise me," I pleaded with my friend, but he was almost gone.

"Listen! Root cellar. She took those things and she's expecting you, Chloe. I have to go," Joey whispered and vanished before our eyes.

"Joey? Can you hear me?" I called up at the ceiling. I was hoping to hear his light footsteps walking across the floor. I heard nothing. "Chloe? Do you feel him anywhere? Please, tell me. Anything at all?" The teenager tilted her head as if she could hear something that I couldn't. I wouldn't doubt it. Chloe was a gifted medium in the truest sense of the word. She squeezed my hand and smiled big.

"Calm down, Aunt Tamara. He's taking a nap. Give him some time. What he did today was huge, and it took a lot out of him. I think it's safe to say that once Joey recovers, he will be stronger than ever." Then her pretty lopsided smile vanished. "Did you hear that?" I listened for a solid minute, but before I could deny hearing anything, I detected a sound.

I heard the clock ticking. I hadn't heard it before, but now, it was ticking as plain as day. Chloe clutched my hand even tighter. It hurt a little, but I clutched hers right back. "The root cellar in the backyard. Do you know where that's at?" Chloe asked me. Her eyes were wide and her face pale.

"I have no idea, but if we are going to have a look, we better get started. Are you sure you're up to this? How is your head?"

The lopsided smile returned. "It feels like something smacked me on the forehead, but I'm not seeing tweeting birds or stars. I don't think it knocked me out, but it stunned me. Let's put these peas back in the freezer and head outside. I can still hear the ticking. How is that possible? Maybe it's in the house. Do you think it could be? I can't locate the sound."

I glanced around, and she was right. I couldn't locate where it was coming from either. It seemed to be all around us, and then it stopped. Goose pimples crept up all over my body, and my flight or fight instincts kicked in. Everything inside of me said I needed to run and take Chloe with me, but where would we go, and how would we get there seeing that I didn't have a vehicle? Not to mention I wasn't much of a runner. I never had been. "I'd feel better if you let me go check it out first. You took a pretty nasty whack to the head, Chloe."

"I won't deny that, but no way am I hanging back." Chloe stripped off her jacket and deposited her purse on the couch.

I had a plan. "We're not going without tools. We're

going to use equipment. We need an EMF detector, the ghost box, and another audio recorder. If you have any protective stones, we could probably use those too."

"I'm on it." Chloe left the room, looking determined. I went to my office and opened the tiny closet. Just the past week, I had repacked my investigator's backpack and stuffed it in here. Better than keeping it in my bedroom closet. Everything I needed was in the backpack, including extra batteries.

My phone began to ring. Talk about bad timing. I sighed as I hit the ignore button.

I'll have to call you back, Angela Webster.

I heard Chloe's footsteps coming down the stairs, and she met me in the doorway. Neither one of us said anything dumb like, "Are you sure about this?"

In this, we didn't have an option. This was do or die for Chloe.

There was no way I was letting Chloe Carol die. Not on my watch.

7

CHLOE

"Any luck over there?" I asked hopelessly, knowing I felt nothing. We had been combing the yard and surrounding woods for a few hours. We were making our way back to the house, and my stomach was grumbling and I was thirsty.

I was ready to call it a day. Whatever was going on inside the Ridaught Plantation refused to be rushed. It was playing games with me, knocking me to the floor and getting in my face. Annabel wanted me to suffer. I would have to be patient and let Annabel lead the way. Maybe Joey got it wrong and the root cellar was in the neighbor's yard. Surely, if there'd been anything like an old underground cellar, we would have uncovered it by now.

Tamara studied the black device in her hand and tapped on the screen with her finger. She shook her head sadly as we continued to pace the yard, hoping against hope we would find the clock, book, and tin. To be fair, the area we walked was huge, and many spots were impenetrable. They were covered with blackberry sticker bushes or clumps of collapsed tree limbs. Coupled with the growing darkness, it made it difficult to spot anything that could potentially lead us to an underground area.

"We should at least try to catch some EVP's," Tamara said hopefully. "If there is a helpful entity around, maybe they can provide us with clues. Just an idea, but it appears to be pretty quiet according to this device."

I pondered her suggestion, but psychically, I felt nothing. There was no one out here living or dead, despite what Joey suggested. The growing darkness gave the neglected yard a menacing feel, and I was ready to retreat inside. For a moment, I could actually see as if I had x-ray vision. I stared up at the Ridaught Plantation, and the family home was completely empty.

"Hey! What are you two doing out here? No wonder you didn't hear me ringing the doorbell. I've been here for five minutes." Kevin walked toward us confidently. He immediately spied the gadget in Tamara's hand and her telltale backpack, which always contained paranormal goodies. "Oh. I see. Anything I should know about?"

Tamara turned off the EMF detector. "Nothing, but things are happening. We think they might be related to the clock Chloe found and the curse. I didn't expect you to return so quickly, Kevin. Any word on my vehicle?"

"I brought you the paperwork you need. It's the official report. Of course, the insurance company will come out and take a look, but it's definitely a total goner. You guys were really lucky. I checked with the manufacturer, and there have been no recalls on that particular vehicle. The fire chief will do a forensic once over, but you may never know why it burst into flames." As usual, Kevin had a file folder in his hand, and he offered it to Tamara.

"Hey, are you hungry? Let's go find some supper, Chloe. I've got lasagna in the freezer. That'll do, right?"

"Sounds like heaven." Kevin grinned, and then his expression changed. "You have a visitor. It looks like your neighbor is heading this way. Pardon me, ladies. I'll go see what she needs," Kevin said as he began to walk toward her. I touched his arm to prevent him. Linda wasn't coming to complain about a screamer or anything like that. Her eyes were fixed on me.

"No. Let me handle this. Lasagna sounds good to me." Tamara waved at Linda, but she and Kevin didn't hang around. The couple went inside and left me with the neighbor, but I noticed Tamara left the back door open. The screen door allowed her to watch me easily from the kitchen. I was right, it was me Linda had singled out. I had been meaning to talk to her. I'd said nothing to Aunt Tamara, but Linda's house was becoming a problem. She was tinkering with things she did not understand or appreciate. Because of her zeal and Linda's clear lack of psychic knowledge, she had initiated some sort of portal in her home. We had a pathway for the dead that ran between our two properties and many of those lost souls found their way into the Dead House. That was bad enough, but Linda was inviting trouble she was not prepared to deal with. With Joey poking around over there all the time, it could make for a dangerous and heartbreaking situation.

"There you are, Chloe. I hope Tamara didn't run off on my account." Linda flashed a pink smile at me and then glanced at the open back door.

"Hi, Miss Linda. She's putting lasagna in the oven. I'm sure she'll be right back." I didn't offer to bring her inside, but I would if she pushed. Linda was a nice lady, just a bit over-talkative and with no respect for personal boundaries. "That nice boy you've been dating came by to see me. I guess he couldn't find you. Y'all been working in the yard?"

With a friendly smile, I deflected her question. I sure didn't want to talk about Trey. "There is definitely plenty to do out here. I haven't seen you out in the yard lately. Those azaleas will be popping out soon. Do you need me to watch Pepe?" Occasionally, I watched her little dog when the couple went out of town for a day or two. He was easy to watch because he didn't like leaving his kennel. Not inside the Ridaught Plantation. He hated the house, but he was a nice enough puppy. The ghost cat found him interesting.

"Yes, if you don't have plans this weekend. Robert is taking me to the casino, and my left hand is itching! I'm sure I'll hit a jackpot. We'll be back before Sunday evening. I'll drop him off tomorrow morning. Pepe's arthritis is acting up, and I don't think he'd enjoy taking a trip to the coast. Oh…I'm feeling something." Linda put the back of her hand to her forehead as if she were an old-fashioned swami receiving a signal from the other side. Willing to give her the benefit of the doubt, I peeked around her large frame while her eyes were closed. There were no spirits. Nothing was around, but a strange air of sadness and desperation that clung to her. What was up with me and auras lately? I'd have to study more about it when I had the chance.

"A loved one will visit you soon. She has an urgent message for you...oh, what is it? The spirits can be so vague. I'm feeling...joy. Like a new baby is coming your way. Yes, that's it! A baby is coming to the house. I am so excited for you all!"

I couldn't help but laugh at her vague psychic prophecy. "Um, okay, but that would be the first I've heard of it. I'm a bit young for kids, Miss Linda. Why don't I come to get Pepe now? That way, you don't have to go to the trouble of bringing him over in the morning. I wouldn't mind having him tonight. He can keep me company while I catch up on math homework. I'll pretend he's my own little baby."

"You don't believe me, I can tell." She made a tsking sound as she shook her over-sprayed hairdo. Her hair never budged, not even on windy days. "They never believe me until it is too late. I don't think the spirits necessarily meant you, young lady. I'll bring Pepe over in the morning, Chloe. Thank you."

With that, Linda Bledsole left me standing in my own backyard, wondering what the heck just happened. She was a weird one, with her fake mediumship and veiled warnings of teenage pregnancy. What a loon. Still, Pepe was a sweet dog.

I walked inside as Kevin and Tamara played domestic. He was searching for dishes while she was chopping up a salad to go with the lasagna. "What did Linda want?"

"Nothing much, just for us to dog-sit Pepe this weekend. I agreed. Poor dog. Oh, and a voice from the other side told her you were going to get pregnant."

"What?" They said it simultaneously.

It was worth passing on the message just to see the look

on their faces. "Don't shoot the messenger. I'm going to take a shower. Back in thirty." I walked out of the kitchen with a big grin on my face as Tamara stopped her chopping and Kevin broke a glass.

Yep, totally worth it.

8

ANNABEL

The boy's broom furiously swept the dirt path before me. By the time the sweaty child completed his task, a few of the petals from my bridal bouquet had fluttered to the ground. I clutched my weary bouquet as I obediently walked the way made for me. My hands trembled. I shook like the proverbial bride on her wedding day, but my heart was as determined and as steady as ever.

This was my destiny!

I would not fret over a few fallen flowers, the lack of a church, or the missing congregation. No matter how expensive those lost petals were and how few the witnesses, I would not allow anything to steal this moment from me.

My walking the aisle with such sweet, rare flowers, tiger lilies, was further testament to Pratt's kind nature. These were magnificent flowers with bright coral-colored petals. Butterflies loved the fragrant flowers, which made them extra special. Perhaps before the ceremony ended, I would see one or two of my beloved monarchs. It would certainly be a good sign, a good omen, and we had been short of those for some time. Betsy loved them too. That much I remembered about my sister. Pratt was a thoughtful man to have recalled that detail. And the trouble he went to bring them here. The bulbs had been carefully packed and sent to Louisiana from Holland of all places. Such luxury!

The elegant piano tinkled a pretty tune as I continued my journey to join Pratt, who stood patiently before the black-robed minister. Pale blue ribbons hung from the two trees that served as our wedding platform. A church wedding would have been more suitable, but the little chapel had burned to the ground a month ago. No one knew why, but many of the old slaves whispered about hoodoo and such. They all believed my mother had been quite mad, and ghosts walked the property after dark.

Although they would not speak of such things to me in front of Anita, I heard their whispers no less. Anita was and remained my strongest defender. She had been more a mother to me than any governess or distant relative. More so than my own mother, who I could not recall having ever held me or comforted me during any distress.

I was often afraid of her in life, doubly so in death.

Our wedding had not been well-favored, quite the opposite. Poor Anita had worked day and night to find good omens for me, bless her soul. She was the last of my family, and she was not even blood-related. With father gone, dead these ten years, I had no one to give me away, hence the boy sweeping. Anita was convinced the activity would circumvent any spirit from clutching my arm and stealing me away from my groom.

Such a romantic yet terrifying notions she had. So very different than the voices in my own head. At least she did not have to hear those. I think sometimes she knew Mother spoke to me. I suspected she could hear her as well, for Anita loved us all. I never confronted her about what she may or may not have heard. We usually kept quiet about Mother. But lately, Anita had spoken quite frequently about the curse that followed Mother from her own family.

It was an old curse and a cruel one. I was determined not to think of curses today.

As if the Lord above agreed with me, a cloud passed over the festivities and bathed us in shadow and coolness for a moment. It skittered away, and the sunshine fell on us all, except Pearl. I noticed with some surprise that the shadow lingered on her face a little longer than the rest of the small gathering. She remembered herself and raised her chin, reminding me to walk with poise and refrain instead of staring at my feet.

Pratt Ridaught stood patiently at the altar, just as he promised. Despite his short stature and full sideburns, which I disliked, he cut a fine figure. I could hardly believe that in a few moments, I would no longer be Miss Annabel Loper, but Mrs. Pratt Ridaught. I would be very happy with a family of my own. Suddenly, as if my thoughts were a beacon, Mother's voice filled my head.

Sons, Annabel. You must have sons. Daughters invite the evil. They initiate the Loper curse. We are all cursed, daughter. You cannot escape it, but your sons can redeem you!

Why did I hear Mother's voice pounding in my ears even today? What madness was this? I refused to entertain a single thought about it. I bit my lip instead of smiling at my groom as I had intended.

To the side stood Miss Pearl Amos, daughter of the late Mrs. Amos, and my dear Pratt's cousin. We, Pearl and I, were not friends, but we would be family soon. She smiled at me to remind me to do the same. She was bossy in that manner. She knew far more about etiquette than I, and I had been looking at the floor preoccupied with tripping and falling over my own feet. I was notorious for doing such things. Anita's fears of impending disaster were influencing me in ways I had not expected.

The truth was that I, Annabel Loper, felt awkward. Even in all my finery, I was far too tall. Someone whispered that about me once and within my hearing no less. That individual had been a friend of Pearl's. So much for etiquette.

Now I would marry Pratt Ridaught. Had there ever been a shorter man? Like me, he was odd and not quite like everyone else, but Pratt had such a big and loving heart.

The poor pastor waited patiently for us to stand before him. I could only imagine what he might have thought about all the strange rituals Anita had added to our wedding ceremony. From the sweeping of the broom to the jumping over it, Pratt and I cared not that these rituals were of African heritage. I loved Anita and would honor her wishes in this matter. I'd had no one else to consult with about my wedding and easily turned to her for her suggestions. I was certain Pearl Amos would have liked to have been in control of my wedding, but I had refused to relinquish the task to anyone.

I was what the world called a spinster, a woman

marrying past her prime. Because I was no nubile young teenager, I could arrange things how I wanted. I wanted to please Anita, and Pratt wanted to please me. That was another reason to love him.

The wedding itself went by so quickly. There was the handfasting with the silky blue ribbons, blue for good luck. Horseshoes hung from the bough above us. Silver rings were exchanged instead of gold, which might incur jealousy amongst lingering spirits, such as Mother or Aunt Lavinia. I had it on good authority she came here too, from time to time. The silver signified peace and prosperity. Pratt offered me a small box of gold coins, which I refused. It was another of Anita's omen tests. By refusing his money, I was proving to the spirit world my love was pure and unbreakable. I thought it was wonderful. Out of the corner of my eye, I saw that Pearl did not share my love for Anita's little touches. She frowned her way through the service.

At the end of the ceremony, we spoke our traditional vows before all the ex-slaves and servants who were present. Because of my family's scandalous past, not many of the local whites wanted to attend any events here at our home. I had expected nothing less. There would be no receiving line, no massive reception with champagne fountains or *petit fours*. We had a simple meal with our few friends, and Pratt and I waltzed together in the fading sunshine to some sentimental tune.

It was that night I heard the clock ticking again.

I knew what clock I heard, for it sounded like no other clock in the house. This clock got louder and ticked faster. Pratt and I had danced until his friends came to fetch him.

They were eager to go outside to smoke cigars and shoot their guns into the dark, up to the heavens. It was another tradition—a local, white one that belonged to the Ridaughts, not me.

As he and his brothers went outside to find a good place to shoot their guns and drink and celebrate the happy day, Anita tugged my hand and pleaded with me to follow her. There were tears in her dark brown eyes. She'd been crying. Her eyes were red and watery. My wedding day should have been a happy occasion, a day to celebrate! Her only daughter of the heart had finally married a good man. That in itself was a miracle.

"I tried to keep this thing away from you, my Annabel. I wanted to burn it and destroy it, but I could not do that. I wasn't sure what she'd done. I don't even like handling it too much. I don't think I can help you anymore, my Annabel. Please forgive me," she said as she faced me, the evil black clock in her hands.

She handed it to me.

Without thinking about it, I received the clock and made no fuss. I did not know what I would do with the monstrous thing. I'd always hated it. Sometimes it played deathly music, a strange precursor to a terrible tragedy. Other times, the clock ticked unnaturally loudly and the dials spun backward. That terrified me more than the music. Why would a clock spin backward? I shivered at the thought as I held the cold item.

It wasn't ticking at the moment, nor were the hands moving. I put it on the mantelpiece in my bedroom and sat on the bed, staring at it as Anita helped me undress.

"I know, child, but I can't keep it from you anymore.

My baby girl, you have to fight for yourself now. You remember all the things I taught you, don't you?" she asked as I picked up my feet and allowed her to untie my satin heels.

"I remember, Anita. Keep the spirits confused. Serve gumbo once a week to appease them. Keep black stones in my pocket to keep the dark ones away. Always burn incense in my bedroom to keep myself safe at night because if she comes, Mother will come at night. I don't understand why she would come. Why could she hate me so much or believe I would continue the family curse?"

Anita helped me remove the layers of skirts and then finally my crinoline. This type of dress was out of fashion, but it was all I had. I had money but no talent for style. Maybe Miss Pearl Amos would be inclined to show me a thing or two. I was certain she wanted to. I would need a wife's wardrobe, especially if we were to travel. I thought that was what we should do. We would leave this place far behind, and I would no more live here.

"I'm sick, child. I'm going to die soon, Miss Annabel. I can no longer help you, child. That clock is yours now. You can't avoid it. It does not hold power over me, but I have been your protector, and it has stolen all my energy. It will do that if you around it too long. Keep it away from your little ones. Never let them see it, Annabel. Keep it away until you can decide what to do with it."

I had mixed emotions about her words. The clock was an ugly thing, but it was a way of feeling connected to Mother and Betsy. I had barely gotten into my nightgown when my husband came into our mutual bedchamber. I snatched the robe and tried to put it on to avoid showing my naked arms.

"That is an ugly thing, isn't it?" he said as he waved Anita out and began untying his cravat. He had no helpers with him, although tradition suggested he could have if he so wanted. I was glad he came alone. Anita averted her eyes as she left. She'd meant to tell me about the ways of men and women, but we'd never got quite around to it. I understood it would require some nudity, but I wasn't sure what to expect or what to do. Immediately Pratt began undressing, and as he did, he kissed me. I quite liked this kiss except for his hairy face. It tickled, and I giggled at the feeling of his fine hairs on my skin. The monarch butterflies had not appeared for my wedding ceremony, but they were certainly in my stomach right then.

The men were outside, still shooting off their rifles while Pratt and I were about to…about to…

Then he kissed me more intensely. His hands began moving over parts of my body no one had touched before. I couldn't think that even my own hands had touched many of those places, and if they had, it was for no such purpose such as pleasure.

Pratt's intensity frightened me, but I did not cry, for that would certainly attract evil spirits. A flood of strange things occurred. I felt a wave of embarrassment at the baring of my breasts, and the lifting of my nightgown. There was a pain when he entered me and the odd wetness he left behind. Thrashing and moaning came from my husband's throat during the strange and unwelcome event. I did not say no. I knew this had to happen. This was what marriage was based on, two people having carnal knowledge of one another. I wondered if this would be every night?

Pratt smoothed my hair and kissed me again, but that was the end of the affection. He soon rolled over, and I was left staring up at the ceiling. The clock began quietly ticking on the wall. At least the numbers ran regularly and not backward. Pratt snored beside me. I wasn't certain if I was expected to sleep in the room with him. I much preferred my own bedroom. I had forgotten that losing my innocence would be accompanied by bleeding. That I did know, but as quickly as it began, it stopped. I would need to bathe for certain. The clock ticked louder as if it knew I was a bloody mess, and it liked it.

What else could I do but keep the thing until I figure out how to get rid of it?

I had an odd idea that maybe I should burn it. After all, the thing was made of wood beneath that lacquer. I used to love watching flames grow. I had dreamed of the church burning, and then it happened. It was as if it had been some sort of prophecy. How else could I explain the premonition? I had told no one about it. Nor did I tell them that matches from my black tin were missing.

I could take the clock out into the woods and burn it!

That's what I'll do, I thought with a smile on my face. I tidied myself with water from the bowl on the table and then sat by the window to enjoy the night air before seeking sleep myself. I would go to bed soon. My husband did snore, and I wondered how I would ever fall to sleep with such a racket.

The groomsmen drank and shot their guns at targets they likely could no longer see. I watched them from the window. They did not see me, but I watched them carrying on as young men do. There were lamps lit, but not enough to lighten up the entire back lawn. One young man in particular, a handsome young man of my husband's acquaintance named Simon, caught my attention. His hair was so blonde I could see it plainly in the increasing moonlight. He was not a local boy, and no one I had ever met before, but I thought him very attractive. Pearl Amos described him as Nordic, whatever that meant. His family was from Sweden.

With my body sore and my mind stirred, I wondered to myself if what I had done with Pratt would have been more enjoyable with Simon. He was tall like me, with a muscled body and light blonde hair. *Did he see me?*

I stepped away from the open window with a pounding heart and crawled back into bed with my snoring husband. I must try to sleep, even if Pratt snored like Porter, the coachman. He had been a large man, old Porter. When they buried him, they had to build an extra-large box for his coffin. Anita missed her husband. He was a kind man.

As I finally closed my eyes and forced Simon from my dreams, I heard a new sound.

No, not a new sound. An old one I had not heard in a while. The sound of the clock, not ticking or whirring backward as it sometimes did. It was playing maniacal, unpleasant music. The sound was so loud and unpleasant Pratt sat straight up in bed and clutched his blanket to his chest. "What in the name of God?"

"It's the clock, husband. I will move it to my room and keep it there, that way you don't have to hear it. I am sorry."

He frowned in the darkness at me, but it was only a hint. "There, there, wife. It is well. Yes, please put it in another room, if you must keep it. Return to bed, my dear. I want to sleep with my wife tonight."

I nodded politely and hurried across the hall to put the clock on my own mantelpiece. It made no other sound. The room was pitch-black and the floor ice cold, even though it had been a hot day. I heard a faint sighing sound as if my bringing the clock here brought someone great pleasure. It was back where it belonged, wasn't it? I scurried out of the room and returned to my husband's bedroom.

I climbed back in bed with Pratt and had nearly fallen asleep when I heard the ticking again. Loud ticking, no whirring. I stared in horror as my eyes adjusted to the light. The clock was spinning backward. I saw it through sleepy eyes as I rose slightly.

I was dreaming. I had to be dreaming! I'd taken the clock to my room and didn't know how it had gotten here. I had placed the clock in the other room for certain. Pratt did not hear it this time. He snored beside me, and soon I settled down beside him and went back to sleep myself, my hand on his arm as a reminder I was not alone anymore. I would be safe with Pratt Ridaught. Safe and happy, despite any ugly old clock.

When I awoke, Pratt, the clock, and my peace of mind were gone.

That was when the tragedies began in earnest.

9

CHLOE

I awoke from my nap with the tune still ringing in my ears. I would never forget that song as long as I lived. The harpsichord ring tone was the same song the music box played during Annabel's time. They were most definitely connected. The last thought I had as I dreamed of Annabel and walking in her shoes, was that the ringing of the clock always brought tragedy.

I regretted waking up from the dream at such a crucial moment, but I was glad to be in my own time and in my own life. There was something off-putting about looking through someone else's eyes and being someone else. I had only assumed someone else's persona a few times. Interacting with ghosts during my sleep always unsettled me. I liked being in control.

That was also the case with my dead ancestor, Annabel. It must run in the family. I sat up and rubbed the sleep from my eyes. *Geez, Louise. What time was it?* I glanced at the alarm clock on the nightstand next to me and was surprised to see an hour had passed. I didn't even recall lying down. I hadn't intended to take a nap, but apparently, I'd needed one, and now I had more information.

The smells of delicious Italian food wafted its way up to the second floor. I quickly changed my clothes and headed down, hoping Tamara and Kevin had left me some lasagna. The thing about frozen Italian food was that it always smelled better than it actually tasted. Occasionally I doctored these bad boys up with a touch of extra garlic powder and Italian seasoning, but I was so hungry right now I didn't care.

As if she read my mind, Tamara called to me from the living room, "We left you plenty! And there's salad!"

"Okay!" I called back as I hurried to make my plate and join them in the living room. The quick glance I had while motoring down the hall assured me they weren't acting all lovey-dovey. Handholding and kissing wasn't something I wanted to see Tamara doing. Not that I believed she was the Virgin Mary or anything, but yuck. I forgot about Linda's warning. I was sure Tamara would fuss at me later for saying what I did in front of Kevin, but I'd thought it was hilarious.

Believe me, I said to myself, we're going to need a laugh when I tell her what I saw in that dream. The ring tone and the clock's tune were exactly the same. I didn't know what to make of it except the need to find the clock grew within me. I didn't know why I would hear the clock and find it only to have it vanish. It was as if the ghost of Annabel were playing some sort of game with me. I didn't understand any of this, I thought as I poured Parmesan on top of a healthy slab of lasagna. I popped the uncovered plate in the microwave. I'd probably get in trouble, but then again, I was the one who cleaned it on a regular basis.

"Hey, did you find everything? What do you want to drink? Coke?" Tamara's voice behind me surprised the heck out of me, but I caught myself before allowing the expletives to fly. I wasn't much of a swearing person, but once I got on a roll, I stayed on one. Lynn was far worse than I was, but neither one of us was pure of mouth.

"You move like a ninja, Tamara. Yeah, I have everything I need. Go be with your company. Try to behave yourself. You heard me pass on what the neighborhood psychic said."

Tamara ignored my attempt to send her back to the living room. She was already filling a glass with ice for me. "I wouldn't put much stock in anything Linda told you. By the way, Angela, the curse breaker is supposed to ride up this evening. She's in town. Can you believe that?"

I removed the hot plate from the microwave carefully and wiped down the inside of the appliance with a damp cloth. *Who's really the neat freak here?* "That's great, and it goes right in line with what happened to me. I don't even remember laying down on the bed, but I took a nap." With the assistance of a folded kitchen towel, I made my way to the table. I could hear the television in the other room, and it sounded as if Kevin were on the phone with someone. That was good because I didn't really want to talk about this in front of him. I couldn't say why except that it was a little embarrassing to admit someone in your family line cursed you. It wasn't like he didn't already know, but I didn't have plans to include him in the resolution.

"Did you have a dream? I dream a lot in this house. Not

lately, thank goodness, but it does seem to bring the most vivid dreams to remembrance. What happened?"

As I began poking at my lasagna, I felt sad and anxious. Sad about what, I couldn't say, but anxious because my secrets, and Annabel's, were about to be revealed to a stranger. Was it even a possibility this curse could really be lifted?

As Kevin continued his conversation in the front room, I described for Tamara everything I had witnessed in my dream. From the young black boy sweeping the dirt in front of Annabel to the red-faced preacher wearing black robes and the short stature of the groom, Pratt Ridaught himself. I told her about the church burning down, the blue ribbons, and the clock and how it came to be in Annabel's possession.

I told Tamara about Annabel's confused thought process and how she grew up believing she was cursed. That Anita, her slave yet also somehow her protector, tried to shield her from its effects.

I told Tamara about the strangeness of Annabel and Pratt's wedding night and how embarrassed Annabel felt about it all. The only thing I left out of my retelling was the incident with Simon.

That encounter, brief as it was, felt so much more private than the actual deflowering of my ancestor. Annabel wouldn't have wanted anyone to know about her feelings for Simon. It wasn't like she would ever see him again. Or maybe she would? I wasn't sure.

Tamara sat speechless as I recounted the sound of the clock's ringing and how it sounded exactly like her phone. "Are you telling me the clock tapped into my cell phone?

And when you hear that song, something bad is going to happen? Is that what you're saying?" Her soft, whispery voice didn't sway my fear that what I was telling her was anything but the truth.

"I can't help but believe those things are connected. The clock, for whatever reason, knows who we are and what we are up to. I wonder what happened to it the morning Annabel woke up and found Pratt missing. Chances are it was probably a misunderstanding. Maybe Pratt took the clock out of the room because he had asked her to move it the night before, and he hadn't been aware it had returned on its own."

Tamara postulated another theory. "Or poor Anita spotted the clock and removed it from the room before Annabel woke up. I guess we won't know unless you continue to dream about Annabel. How do you feel about that? Psychic dreaming, I mean. Is it safe?"

I pierced the lasagna with my fork as she asked me her question. I nibbled on it, and as expected, it was pretty tasteless. "Yeah, I think so. I am looking forward to meeting this Angela Webster person. I've never met a curse breaker before. Have you?"

"Not directly, but I know your mother has, and she was very impressed. She described them as a very dedicated group of individuals. I mean you'd have to be, right? She talked about two who impressed her, and she worked with them in the past. One was associated with a residential haunting, and the other was to combat a curse attached to a jail. Angela Webster came highly recommended by my former community." Kevin called Tamara's name and she answered, "Be there in a minute." She slid a paper towel to me and glanced at her oversized watch. "She should be here in about fifteen minutes or so if she doesn't get lost out here in the boondocks. It's easy to do on roads that aren't marked well, especially if you're not familiar with where to turn. I better go see what's going on with Kevin. I have a suspicion he just got called back into work. Love you, Chloe."

"I love you too, Aunt Tamara. Thanks for dinner."

She left me alone with my pitiful lasagna, and I tried doctoring it up so I could finish eating it. A couple of sprinkles of seasoning put it right. I gobbled the gooey food and went for the salad.

Luckily for me, I didn't have to work anytime soon. My boss had called to let me know she hired a new girl who was getting her training hours this weekend. There went all the good hours. That's what happens when the new girl is the boss's niece. It wasn't like I had to work, but I did enjoy the job. At least it got me out of the Dead House for a little while, but working ten hours a week wasn't going to cut it. Now, with the car situation, it was probably a good thing I wasn't on the schedule. Once we got this curse thing settled, I would have to look for something else. Tamara was right. I could afford to buy a car. I didn't know why I was being so timid about it.

"Psst! Is it all clear?" Joey's head popped around the corner, and I was surprised to see he had a suitcase in his hand, an actual suitcase. One I'd seen in the attic if I wasn't mistaken.

"Joey? Where are you going?"

"I have to go, Chloe. The Reaper is back, and he's not happy with you. He wants a soul, and I'm not ready to go!

Don't tell Tamara!" For someone who was trying to be quiet, he was as loud as a living person with his jangling bracelets and ridiculous outfit. He wore his usual blue jeans but had on a pair of wedges and a goofy tank top. At least they weren't my clothes.

"In the house?" I rose from the table, fearing for Joey. I didn't want him to get captured either, and I could believe that the Reaper would want him. "Did you see him in the house, Joey?"

"Yep. At the end of our hallway, where we used to see him. He is in the house, and he is chanting or something. I swear to God, he said my name! I'm not ready to go, and when I do, it won't be with the Reaper. Promise me, Chloe, that you will help me move on when it's time. When I'm ready." He put his suitcase on the floor and nervously shifted his Doo rag. He was clutching it as if it were a life preserver as he waited to hear my promise. I wasn't sure I had any control over that, but I told him I would do my very best to protect him.

"Shouldn't you at least tell Tamara yourself? Am I supposed to do it? Where are you going anyway?"

"I can't face her, besides she's outside with her boy toy kissing him goodbye. Quick, give me a pen. I'll write her a note."

"Really? You can write?"

"No, idiot. Of course not. It's taking everything I have to hold on to this suitcase. You'll have to tell her."

"Always running. I don't think the Reaper can actually collect you, Joey. If he could, he would have already, I'm sure of it. Just stay here and chill out. I'll tell you what. Linda Bledsole asked me to watch Pepe for her this weekend. She's not going to be home. Robert is going too. Stay here until she leaves, and then hide out over there."

"That might work, but I don't want to be here when this other character shows up—Angela or whoever she is. I have a bad feeling."

"You always have a bad feeling. She's a curse breaker, not a psychic. She can't make you leave. I think we'll have some answers soon, Joey. Unpack your bag, and you can stay in my room if you're so worried about it, but just for tonight, and no sleeping in my bed. You're too cold. Tomorrow you can go next door and haunt the parakeet."

He snorted. "Ha-ha, very funny. This is on you, Chloe Carol. Take care of it. I'll stick around, but I'm keeping my bags packed. So can I go to your room? Do I have your permission?"

I picked up my dishes and looked him squarely in his luminous eyes. "Yes, you have my permission, but it is only temporary, and you can't invite friends over to hang out in there. No one. Not even the cat."

"Fine. Have it your way. Thanks, Chloe. I'll go make myself comfortable."

His wedges tapped on the floor as he walked back down the hall with his dusty suitcase.

"Not too comfortable, it's only for one night!" I yelled back at him. "Hey, what about the root cellar?" I'd meant to ask him, but he was mumbling as he went upstairs. I would talk to him tonight after the curse breaker left.

I'd pick his brain, whether he wanted me to or not. He would be staying in my room for a night and could at least tell me what I wanted to know.

As I washed my dishes, I heard Kevin's car pulling out.

Date night had come to a sudden end. It must be tough dating a cop.

I put the dishes in the drying rack and turned to go seek out Tamara when I paused. I thought for a second, I heard ticking. As quickly as I discerned it, it faded into the background noise along with the ice maker and the air conditioning, which had kicked on.

"Chloe, company's here!" Tamara called to me from the foyer. I put on a smile and folded the dishtowel before going to join her and the curse breaker.

This should be interesting.

10

TAMARA

I stood inside the open door and watched a tiny red car pull into the driveway. My boyfriend headed in the opposite direction. Kevin didn't waste any time leaving. He had received some sort of emergency message from dispatch. The guy who was supposed to be on call was nowhere to be found, so that left Kevin to go and investigate whatever the emergency call was about.

I never really thought much about what he did for a living, not anymore, but at times like this, I could see how someone would think twice before getting involved with anyone in law enforcement. It was certainly stressful thinking and imagining horrible situations. I didn't say anything like, "Call me when you know something." Part of his job was to know things and not tell others about what transpired in the sleepy little town of Crystal Springs. I did hope to hear from him soon, though.

Angela could've been a Tupperware salesperson by the look of her. She was older than me, but not by much. She had a sassy haircut—a cute stacked bob—conservative clothing, and a friendly way about her. I was relieved, but then I reminded myself that you could not judge a book by its cover. Just because Angela Webster wasn't covered in jailhouse tattoos and seemed to have all of her teeth didn't mean she was trustworthy. She had come highly recommended by friends in the paranormal community, but I had never met her before. We'd only interacted through email and phone.

"You must be Tamara. I'm Angela. Are you guys ready for me?" Angela offered up a friendly wave as she headed toward us. Chloe snuck up behind me, and to my surprise, I heard Joey's heels clogging up the staircase. That wasn't like him. He was usually right in the middle of everything, but he was making himself scarce for some reason.

I noted that Angela didn't bring any materials with her, but her hand went into her cross-body purse. She retrieved a tiny bottle of lotion or something with which she used to rub her hands. She studied the house and us but did not come up the steps right away. *What's the hold-up, lady?*

"Yes, I am Tamara, and this is Chloe. Come on inside, make yourself at home." She continued to rub her hands furiously and then adjusted the strap on her purse and lighted up the stairs like she had no hesitation at all.

"Very nice to meet you both. What a lovely old place. It's alive, isn't it? Are we the only ones here?"

I didn't know how to respond to that question. Well, they say honesty is the best policy. I might as well try a little of that.

I stepped back and made room for Angela to come inside. "We do have a ghost in the house, but he is more a family friend than any sort of troublemaker. His name is

Joey, and we don't want anything we do tonight or any other time to harm him." Chloe agreed with me then offered her hand to Angela, who accepted it and stepped inside.

Her curious expression didn't surprise me. I don't know how I would respond if someone told me they had a house ghost. Not that Joey was a pet. He was a member of the family.

"I thought I sensed another energy here, but I wasn't getting that it was a ghost. I'm not here to deal with ghosts or any entity. I'm here to help you with your curse. It's a troubling one, isn't it?" She rubbed her hands again before coming in. I thought it must be a curse breaker ritual. She seemed friendly enough. "Mattie was right about you, Tamara Garvey. You're stunning. I'm surprised you're not doing some sort of modeling. I could see that. Hi, Chloe. Those eyes of yours. You've heard of old souls? That's a real thing, you know. I think you may be one of them, but that's just my first impression. My, what a wonderful yet chilling atmosphere." Angela walked deeper into the foyer and made a puffing sound with her lips.

"How well do you know Mattie? I haven't seen her in ages." I closed the door and shoved my hands in my jean's pockets. Suddenly, I felt tired. I wondered if maybe I should have suggested she come in the morning.

Angela continued her survey of the front of the house and answered me absently. "We've been on at least a hundred investigations together, mostly in Florida. I keep getting drawn there. I guess it's fate. I'll have to move there one day. Just to save on mileage and gas." She laughed, but I could tell she still had her feelers out and she was searching for something. None of us spoke as she touched things, the table, the chair, the wall. I was always curious to learn how other folks in the paranormal field worked with the supernatural. Chloe grabbed my hand and held it like a child. I squeezed her slender fingers.

"What did you mean when you called me an old soul?"

Angela stopped her surveillance and faced Chloe. I noticed they were about the same height. Angela's soft expression spoke volumes. She had great empathy for Chloe and what she was going through. I could see it in her eyes, and I was grateful. "Some souls have specific destinies. I think you are one of those souls, Chloe Carol. Before I met you, I sensed that about you. Maybe that means you are the one who was always destined to break this curse."

"Do you want to see more of the house?" I asked, hoping to move this process along. I was eager to see Angela work.

"No, I don't need to see anything. Just Chloe, and you, of course. As her guardian, I would like you to sit in on our first session. I might need your help."

"Help with what?" Chloe asked as she released my hand and glanced at the two of us as if we were plotting something heinous, like an exorcism.

"Relax, kiddo. I'm not going to do anything at all tonight. I just want to talk with you. Is there a quiet place where we can do that?" That last question was for me, and I offered up the living room with its floppy cushions and comfy couch. Angela removed her purse and put it on the couch beside her. Funnily enough, she sat in Joey's spot. Good thing he wasn't down here. He might have something to say about that. People normally avoided his spot on the couch.

"Tell me about you, Chloe Carol. Before we talk about curses and haunted houses and all the other things you have going on, tell me about you," said Angela.

"I'm nothing special. I'm a senior in high school, and I'm a medium. Dead people like talking to me, but I didn't know that until I moved here. This is my family's home, but I don't know much about it. My room is on the second floor. It's like my own apartment up there. I like it. No offense to Aunt Tamara. She's awesome. I'm just kind of independent."

Angela leaned back and got comfortable as she half turned on the couch. I was sitting in the slouchy chair beside them. "Tell me about you and your mother. Were you close? Have you been able to reach her, since you're a medium?"

Chloe swallowed and shook her head. "Not without Joey's help. I've seen her, but it's a struggle. Annabel, our ancestor, wants to keep us apart. She hates her own bloodline, and I don't understand that."

"But you've seen Annabel? Interacted with her?"

"Yes, in a dream. The interaction wasn't the same as when I deal with regular dead people. She doesn't just come to me and ask for help. She doesn't want to move on or find her lost dog. Annabel doesn't want anything from me except to end the family line. I suspect, and I can't prove this, but from what I've seen with Annabel and her mother, I think insanity runs in my family." Chloe's damp eyes broke my heart. I tugged a tissue out of the box beside me and passed it to her. "I don't want to be crazy, y'all. I don't want to die because of a curse. I guess…no. I'm not guessing. I am seriously hoping not to die. And what happens when I have kids? Are they doomed? Did the curse take Mom out, and maybe my grandmother?" Then she began to shake with sobs. It was unlike Chloe to fall apart in front of anyone. Immediately, I sat on the edge of the couch and put my arm around her.

"It's okay, baby girl. I'm sorry. I'm sorry for all of this." I closed my eyes and held her to me. By the time she was done crying, my jeans were soaked with her tears, and half the tissue box had been emptied. All three of us were crying. What a heartbreaking situation for a teenager to endure.

Angela spoke softly. "It's a strong curse. Generational curses often are. Because they are so old, it has had plenty of time to grow, but we *can* break it. It will take hard work, but I can see that you are committed and you are strong. Yes, Chloe. Look at me. Inside of you is all the power you need. I'm just here to guide you. I'll need you to make me a list."

"A list?" Chloe patted her eyes with the ragged tissues, but she was hanging on to Angela's every word.

Angela nodded. "Yes. Make a list of every way you think this curse has manifested so far. Anything you can attribute to Annabel. Bad luck events. Seeing black shadows. Strange activity you would not attribute to a ghost, and I do believe you know the difference."

Chloe's eyes lit up. "I keep journals of everything. How soon do you need this list?"

"As soon as you can get it to me. Tomorrow will be fine.

I'm looking for patterns in the manifestations, clues to how it operates."

Chloe glanced up at me, and I quietly took my seat back in the slouchy chair. "We have to tell you about the clock. It's a new development in this story."

"Clock?" We nodded, and Angela's eyes narrowed.

"Interesting. Tell me about Annabel and this clock. I still want the list, but let's not wait. Let's not wait another minute."

In a rush, Chloe let it all go. The dreams, the interactions with the ghost of Annabel, and Mrs. Loper. She explained the discovery of the clock, the book, and the tin. It was emotional but also appeared therapeutic for her. At the end of her spontaneous presentation, Chloe took a deep breath and leaned back on the couch. Her slender body sagged as if she'd just dropped a heavy emotional load.

"Do you still think we can break it? It's a lot, isn't it?"

"It sounds like, and this is just an initial observation, I won't really know until I start doing the untangling. It sounds like this clock is a power object—a magically charged item used to facilitate the curse. The book is probably a key, but heaven knows what is in that tin. You have two spirits at war over you. One wanted you to find the clock, and the other wanted to hide it. And it did."

I gasped at the idea of a spiritual war happening around Chloe. "Joey isn't involved, is he?"

"Only as a sympathetic friend. Let him go, Tamara. You too, Chloe. Let him leave so he doesn't get caught in Annabel's web. He's in her dimension and on her plane. He's too accessible to her. You hear me, Joey? You are listening. He's always listening, isn't he? I like him, but we need to clear the place before we go to battle."

I used to think clearing a space meant burning sage and sprinkling a place with salt. Angela had other things in mind. "You'll need to clean the place, top to bottom. I mean, scrub every surface. Call a friend to help."

"What?" The place wasn't dirty. I wasn't a poor house-keeper. "Really?"

"It's a symbolic gesture. It shows intent and will help us when the real battle begins."

Chloe volunteered and promised Lynn would help, too. "Besides a list, what else can I do?"

"Tomorrow evening I'm going to help you slip into a trance. It's the easiest way for me to see Annabel. I know that's asking a lot. You don't know me at all, but I promise you I won't let you go too deep. Tapping into your vision of Annabel will help me weigh her strength, and that's important."

Chloe immediately agreed with Angela's request. "I'll do whatever you need me to do. You really think it's possible? We can break it?"

"Yes, I do, but I must warn you. There is a small chance we won't break it, and an even greater chance it will get worse before it gets better."

"Worse than the car bursting into flames? Or chande-liers falling to the floor?"

Angela's steely gaze met mine. All her previous softness vanished for a few seconds. "Oh, yes. Much worse. Let's get to work ladies. You have your tasks, and I have mine. I will call you in the morning, but if anything happens, reach out to me. I'll be available."

She rose from the couch as we did. She held her bright pink purse in her hands as she hugged us both, and then we walked her to the door. After Angela left, Chloe and I sighed, thinking about the chore ahead of us.

We had a house to clean. Chloe had a list to make. I felt completely overwhelmed. We worked deep into the night, and I finally passed out smelling like bleach and disinfectant. I had totally forgotten about Kevin and his emergency call. My body was tired, and my brain mushy.

At some point in the night I woke up, but only momentarily. Joey's translucent lips brushed my forehead, and he mumbled something about going on vacation. I woke up wondering if I'd dreamed it, despite the weird cold spot on my forehead.

Chloe came into my room and crawled into bed with me. She brought her blanket because she and I both were cover-hogs. "He's gone, Tamara."

I wanted to cry, to say something in protest, but I fell back asleep. I woke up to the sound of a barking dog. *Oh, great. Pepe was here. I'll have to clean the house again before noon.* I swung back the covers feeling exhausted and went to greet my day.

It was going to be an interesting one.

11

ANNABEL

The girls ceased their singing and handclapping, and the brief silence was a relief. My daughters were always chattering, giggling, and whispering about heaven knows what. Most likely me, their unfortunate mother.

Amie had a lovely singing voice, but she was too shy to perform on request. Not that we had too many visitors nowadays. We were practically imprisoned here. Only Pratt got to leave whenever he wanted to. At the drop of a hat, he would leave for a ride or for business. I wondered what that felt like, to abandon all responsibilities and spend time in the sunshine. How long had it been since I'd ventured out?

Amie sang a few notes from her songbook as Daisy instructed her. Amie's beautiful voice might lead her to great things. On the other hand, Jemima would sing with abandon, and rarely did her voice land on the right note. I bit my lip to hide a mocking smile. Mothers were not supposed to have favorites. Not like my mother. I would never be like her.

The girls were now flocking around their father, who enjoyed being the center of attention. Amie cast a wary eye in my direction, but Jemima ignored me. My youngest daughter only ever thought about silliness and having a good laugh. Too bad she didn't apply such focus to her studies. It was a sad thing to be an uneducated girl in times such as these. At least she could learn to spell her name correctly. At the rate her father was spending our money, she would not have much to offer a husband beside a sparkling personality. Amie and Jemima needed an education.

Of the three of my children, my son remained perpetually aloof from my husband. His disdain for Pratt's ridiculous stories was obvious. It was Mitchell who held my heart the closest. I loved him so much it made my arms ache to think I could no longer hold him. I missed him being a baby I could dandle on my knee. Baby Mitchell's infectious laugh brightened every gloomy day. He was too big for petting anymore, or so Pratt complained to the point I obeyed him.

I loved Mitchell so much my heart ached when I gazed at him for too long. I could see so much of his father in him. It was still a wonder to me no one else did. My son was fair-haired, like his sisters, but that was where the similarities between the siblings ended. My daughters had dark brown eyes like Pratt and all the Ridaught family, but Mitchell's eyes were blue. Sky blue like heaven.

On occasion, I caught Pratt staring at Mitchell oddly and also at me, but there was no confrontation and no accusation. Just silence. However, Pratt did not come to my bed anymore, and for that, I was relieved. My last pregnancy had almost killed me, and the doctor had warned Pratt what another pregnancy might mean for me. Whether he took him seriously out of love for me or revulsion because of my unfaithfulness, I could not say.

Mitchell was the spitting image of his father in every way, and one day there would be no denying it to anyone. I would do anything to keep him safe. Most recently, safe from sickness and the fever. I knew how deadly fever could be because it had taken my sister after long days of torture. When the sickness began ailing the servants, I evacuated nearly the entire top floor of the house to protect Mitchell while he recovered. My daughters, too, but they were not as delicate as my son. They were short and sturdy, like Pratt.

I'd already lost Simon. I couldn't bear to lose Mitchell too. I would not allow that to happen. Not if it was in my power.

Daisy's pretty laughter stirred me out of my private memories of warm, stolen afternoons in the arms of my now-dead lover. To think he was dead. Simon was dead and, in the cold, cold, ground. It was too much to bear. It had been impossible to hide my grief when I first heard the news. I disappeared into my bedroom, claiming some sickness or another, but it had been a ruse. I could not allow myself to wail like a banshee and offer up savage screams of despair. For me, there could be no overt displays of grief, no ripping of the wallpaper, or covering the mirrors as I wanted. I cried a river of tears over him.

It did not bring him back, but it did push me further away from my husband. He barely glanced in my direction these days, but my daughters were always in his lap or leaning over him. Laughing. Living. Loving their father.

Pratt spread his map book on his desk. I guess one could say he was educating the children and the new governess on the dangers of travel. Great sea monsters lurked in the Pacific Ocean, a body of water so large it covered half the world. Chunks of ice, as large as houses, drifted in the northern sea. The ice was such a problem that captains could not guide ships to the top of the world. Daisy's breathy voice questioned him about one thing and then another.

Such a silly girl.

As usual, Pratt had an answer for every one of the girl's questions. Oh yes, he knew everything about shipping, even though I knew he had never taken the briefest of voyages. His family certainly knew all about shipping, but not my husband. He was the son of a shipping magnate, a son who had not been selected as heir to the massive Ridaught fortune. He received a pittance compared to the rest.

Pratt's self-importance grew great, but unfortunately, he had no trade. The days of making a living as a gentleman were over. One had to do more than collect rent from a few farmers to be a success. I said as much to him in one of our last disagreements. I knew he was squandering my fortune, but there wasn't much I could do about it. What would I do if he told the world the truth about Mitchell? I must keep my mouth closed and endure.

Daisy's black ribbon shook at the back of her head as she agreed with my husband on some unimportant matter. Pratt smiled up appreciatively before he leaned over his map with his magnifying glass. Those bushy sideburns had specks of gray in them, but to some women, including the inexperienced Daisy Mixon, they were considered attractive. I used to love Pratt. I had believed the day I accepted him for my husband. Walking down the dirt path, standing with him under the trees, the blue ribbons hanging from the branches above us, I had loved him deeply. Or so I had believed.

That was before I knew what he was doing: stealing from my children and me.

Before I knew real love with Simon.

I realized at that moment how much I hated Pratt, and it took my breath away. I hated that he was alive, and Simon was not. How was this fair?

The children gathered around the desk, completely enamored with my husband's incredible sea tales. Like their young governess, they willingly accepted every word that fell off their father's lips as the truth. In their eyes, he could do no wrong.

At least Mitchell avoided him. I had not intentionally cultivated such a separation between the boy and his supposed father, but it had occurred, nonetheless. How could I know who was to blame? Mitchell sat propped up in the window, his face leaning against the glass pane. As always, his hair was carefully combed, his angular, handsome face clean, and his boots were polished. Mitchell always took such good care of himself and with no harassment from me. Not like my daughters, who frequently resisted hair brushing and bathing.

Mitchell's attention was captured by something outside the window, but there were no trees near the glass.

Nothing was close to that particular window, but there was a definitive slapping sound. The wind blew fiercely. I could hear the eaves of the house squeaking as the air shifted.

Slap, slap, slap.

It sounded like a branch. "Mitchell? What do you see, son?" I whispered to him as I quietly closed my book and left it on the cushion beside me. His favorite perch, the window box, had an expansive view of the property on sunny days. I smiled as I strolled toward him, but he didn't seem to hear me, nor did he shift his attention from the scenery. His mouth was open slightly as if he were staring in awe at something. What could possibly be of such fascination to him? Before joining him, I glanced over my shoulder. It was not my desire to draw attention to us. The girls and Pratt did not appear to notice anything unusual.

Let Mitchell and I be forgotten by all of them. Leave us alone, I thought jealously. The gathering did not notice the odd tapping against the glass, but Mitchell's eyes would not be swayed. His mouth even wider and his face grew pale, which troubled me deeply.

"Mitchell?" I asked as I walked with purpose to my son, my heels making comfortable thumps on the carpeted floor. I didn't bother smoothing the wrinkles out of my gray skirts. Pratt didn't bother scolding me about my appearance now that Daisy Mixon arrived. I was relieved about that. For the life of me, I didn't recall agreeing to the hiring of a governess, no matter what he said, but if it kept him from my bed, so much the better.

"Mitchell?" I asked again, my smile fading as I closed in on him. An inky black silhouette covered half the window. By the hair and slender shoulders, the figure belonged to that of a woman, but the darkness made it impossible to see her face. Her palms were flat, her fingers splayed, her face pushed next to the glass. I muffled a moan as I took in the unearthly sight. My mind twisted and raced as it searched toward a possible solution. How on earth was this possible? What could stand this tall? We were on the second floor, and there was no tree, nothing to support a climber.

Tap, tap, tap. The long, slender fingers of the dirt-covered creature tapped purposefully on the window. I stared in horror although my mind screamed, "Grab the child! Protect the child!"

The rain came down, and the thing stepped back from the window. One step, then two. The rain came down heavier as if she had called it, her own to command. Sheets of rain fell when minutes ago there had only been the sun.

The rain fell, and the creature turned. It's bare white arm, long and spindly, showed briefly before it melted into the rain.

Behind me, the sound of a woman screaming shocked me into action. It wasn't Jemima or Amie, but Daisy the governess who shrieked in horror. I pulled Mitchell to me and covered his ears with my hands, but it was impossible to drown out her screams.

Then I realized I was screaming with her.

1 2

———

ANGELA

"I was wondering when I would hear from you, Angela. It's been a while. How have you been?" Just hearing Claude's smooth voice in my ear erased much of my current anxiety. I knew that would be the case. Claude had a way about him. Not so much charm, more like unearthly confidence. Confidence in himself, and also in the people around him. He had always been good at seeing the best in others. Back when we spoke more frequently, he would say to me, "The only thing you lack is a good memory. Remember your victories, Angela. They are the keys to unlocking your future. You always forget them and too easily."

I smiled, even though he could not see me. "I think this curse is tied to an object, Claude. Not only that, but it is deeply generational. I may be over my head with this one."

He sighed deeply, his disappointment obvious. It was nice to know I could still disappoint him, I thought sourly. "No formalities then. Right to the point. That saddens me, Angela. Nevertheless, I am willing to share my thoughts on the matter. Tell me all that you know, all you've experienced."

Ignoring his sad tone, I began to explain what I meant. I relayed all the information I could about the clock, the way it was described to me, and about Chloe Carol, the girl who inherited it all. The house, the curse, the ghosts. The many, many ghosts.

"This Tamara, she is not the child's blood relative?" Claude asked. His voice sounded a bit crackly for a moment. The connection could break at any moment. There was no promise I would be able to reach him again. Claude kept his own mind, even now. Even after all this time.

"In this day and age, young women her age are not referred to as children. No. Merely a friend of the family. Chloe's late mother was her best friend. I like the child, as you call her. She's intelligent, spiritually sensitive, and independent. Yes, I like her."

"Meaning you are going to help her no matter what I say."

"That's not fair, Claude. I do want to help her, though. She's haunted, doubly so because of her abilities and the house and everything. It's really quite a testament to her strength to have endured this long without losing her life or soul."

I heard the sound of crashing waves. Was Claude near the beach? He loved the ocean and would have lived there if I had agreed to such a thing. Living by the beach seemed such an impractical thing. All those hurricanes, storm surges, sharks...

"Some curses cannot be broken, dearest."

Twisting my hair around my finger, I paced the hotel room as I listened. "You know I don't agree with that, Claude. There is no such thing as an unbreakable curse."

He chuckled softly. I could imagine his white teeth and lovely smile. "If you were a Kennedy or a Kline, you might feel differently. I love you, but you are wrong." His offhand declaration of love hurt, but I wouldn't allow him to distract me so easily.

"I'm never wrong," I said smugly. I didn't really believe that. I was merely parroting what Claude had said for years. He both craved and disliked being challenged intellectually. It was a strange dichotomy.

"You are wrong now, Angela. Let me come there. Let me join you. I can help," he said with a burst of exuberance.

I shook my head and declined his offer. "That's not possible. I won't allow that." A quiet pause passed between us. When the sounds of the crashing waves faded, I thought perhaps we'd been disconnected, but then I heard his voice. Soft and warm and silky.

"I love you, Sparrow. I would never harm you. Please reconsider. I would never hurt you." I flushed at his pleas, but they did not move me. Too much had happened between us. Despite his caramel sounding voice and deep understanding of the subject matter, I would not allow myself to trust him. Maybe he forgave me. Maybe he did not. I was too tired to spar with him. It was best to change the subject. He would understand what I was doing, but I hoped he wouldn't push me.

"You know I hate that name. Nobody calls me that except you. I should never have told you about it. I'd like to leave those days behind."

As expected, he laughed again. "I love that you hate it. Tell me more about your case. I am anxious to see how you solve this mystery since you're going to be stubborn. No such thing as unbreakable curses indeed."

I let that go. "They have an interesting ghost at the Ridaught Plantation. He's very active. I think his energy has helped make this curse stronger. I don't believe it's intentional, but he draws energy from the two women. They are like batteries, the younger is stronger and more in tune with her own energy. Tamara prefers to use her gifts through traditional tools."

"What kind of tools?"

"The traditional ghost hunting kind. Digital recorder, the radio frequency box, the IR camera. She doesn't need these things at all. She's intuitive, but also ignorant in a way. Chloe is a different story altogether. This ghost is attached to them both. I think he knows how this will pan out, and he's choosing a side."

Claude whistled softly. "I hope that's not the case and you're wrong about that."

"Yeah, me too. I hope I'm wrong. I don't think they would agree to banish him. He's like a member of their family. The Ridaught Plantation pulsates with power. Neutral power, too. It could go either way, Claude. If the place will belong to the light or to the darkness, that's going to depend on them. I am getting started tonight. I need to prepare."

"Be careful."

"That goes without saying. It's hardly likely I'll be careless." I snorted as I began unpacking my bag.

Claude's quiet voice was hard to hear. "Well, dearest. Love makes you say stupid things. Pardon me."

I couldn't ignore his love declaration again. "This is the third time tonight you've told me you loved me. Why, Claude? It's not like you to be so vocal about your feelings. What's the occasion?"

"You act as if you don't trust me, and that hurts, Angela. I noticed you have not returned my affections at all. What am I to make of that?"

"Claude, why now, when you know that neither of us can act upon it? I better say goodbye. I'm going to be at this for a couple of hours."

He had no answer for me except to say, "Use caution. Good night, Angela. Think of me when you enter your dreams."

"Good night, Claude. I will hold off on dreams for now, as much as that is within my power. I wish you well." I sagged on the bed as our link weakened and my late lover disappeared into the void. It drained me reaching out to him, but I had been selfish. I had been hungry for Claude's assurance, and my need had given him access to me at a time when I did not need to be vulnerable.

Ah, Claude DeMoyne! You will always be my weakness.

After a few minutes and many unshed tears, I finished unpacking my bags. I would be here a few days at least, maybe longer. I put the items I needed in particular on the small round table in the suite. I would try the easy things first, and then hopefully, we wouldn't need a dangerous intervention. I prayed I would not need Claude. I scribbled some notes in my tiny notebook.

Curse confirmed, generational in nature, tied to an object or objects. Active site.

I began to map out a course of action. I'd seen a creek near the Ridaught Plantation. That was the perfect place to do a water cleansing, and Chloe would need one. The water might be slightly chilly this time of year, but it could be a good place to start.

I scribbled a few more notes.

Selenite and bay for cleansing and breaking. Should repeat at sunup and sundown. Reflection work won't be possible. The spell caster is dead. Unless...no, that's dangerous. Too dangerous to even consider. What am I thinking?

I tossed the pen on the notebook and walked to the tiny refrigerator as if some kind, benevolent housecleaning fairy might have left me a few snacks. I would need to go to the grocer for a few things. I filled a cup with water, took a sip and put the cup in the mini sink. Yuck. The water here was terrible. I definitely needed bottled water and crackers. I did love carbs when I worked out these things.

I reached for my purse and room key and looked up just in time to see the papers of my notebook fluttering. The air conditioning unit wasn't on, and there were no windows open. Even the bathroom door was closed. There was no reason for a draft.

No reason for the papers to shuffle like that.

I walked over to the table and gazed down at the scrawled warning. Oh yes. This was a clear message. One word had been scribbled over my notes. Large letters were scratched deeply into the paper, so deeply I was surprised it hadn't torn up the pages. Someone had drawn it over and over again. I had only been gone a few seconds.

I touched the paper and rubbed the word with my finger.

WITCH

I closed the notebook and put the pen in my purse. I left the hotel and went on my supply run with renewed determination. There was no timeline. I would stay as long as it takes. If this entity thought it would deter me with a little name-calling, then it had much to learn. I was not one to run for the hills at the slightest scare.

Still, it was unsettling that an entity so strong could find me so easily. It meant my barriers were down and my defenses too weak to keep this strong spirit at bay. It knew I was coming and it didn't like that at all. I knew why. Claude! I should never have allowed him access to my mind. My moment of weakness might have cost me much more than what I'd already paid.

Did this mean the curse had a consciousness? Oh God! Please, don't let that be true. I left the hotel room in search of a grocery store and, hopefully a metaphysical shop.

Time to go to battle.

13

TAMARA

Pepe barked at us from the window. I scowled at him as I pulled the EMF detector out of my backpack. If his yapping didn't deter the ghosts, Chloe's noisy ringtone would. It was a good thing the element of surprise wasn't necessary for paranormal investigation.

"What if she comes while we're gone, Tamara? Shouldn't we leave her a note on the front door?" Chloe shoved her phone in her back pocket, but who knew how long that would last. Teens and their phones. She rubbed her hands nervously on her jeans. Chloe was as nervous as a cat in a room full of rocking chairs.

"I left her a voicemail. I don't understand what's keeping her. I would have thought she'd have been here by now. Anyway, I say we stick to the plan. Let's try to recover that clock. You and I both know it's out there. Joey wasn't making that up."

There was every possibility we would notice fluctuations in the EMF field that would lead us to the item. I felt certain we would be able to locate the spot. At least the paranormal ticking stopped.

I guessed that was a good thing.

We walked slowly. I kept a watchful eye on Chloe, whose anxiety appeared to be reaching max levels. She was muttering to herself but didn't turn to go back to the house. Chloe paused every few feet and scanned the area around her. Maybe she was using her abilities to home in on the clock.

The EMF detector lit up like a Christmas tree. It went from light green to yellow to bright red. I tapped on the side of the machine so we could hear the audio, too. *Ping. Ping. Ping.* It hung in the red for a few seconds and then stopped altogether. Whatever passed us had moved quickly, and it was strong enough to move the levels.

"What just happened?" Chloe asked as she whirled around slowly, her fingers spread out, her eyes watching the ground. "Did you see that?"

"I saw the K2 meter bounce. What did I miss? Did you see something?" The pink-cheeked teenager did not answer me but took off walking in the opposite direction.

"This way!" Chloe shouted as I followed after her.

"Watch your walking!" The EMF was screaming, and my heart was pounding as I hurried behind Chloe through the tall grass. I'd meant to have the lawn care people come, but I hadn't gotten around to it yet. Too little time, too many ghosts.

The machine in my hand began to vibrate, and the light pinged to full red. I was confused. This instrument didn't have a vibration setting, just lights and noise. If it did, I would've known about it. I had used this kind of machine and this particular brand for many years. I'd been on dozens of paranormal investigations with no vibrating handhelds. I wanted to drop the machine on the ground, but I was terrified, and I couldn't slow my pace. I had to keep up with Chloe.

"Hurry up, Tamara! We are getting closer! I can feel it!" Suddenly Chloe stopped with her arms out, her hands in fists. Out of the corner of my eye, I saw a wisp of white. The movement reminded me of my childhood when my mother put the sheets on the clothesline and a pop of wind caught it in a good breeze.

Don't be so dramatic, Tamara. There are no breezes out here today. In fact, it's hot. Too hot.

I stood beside Chloe, looking for whatever it was she thought she discovered. I didn't see anything, but sometimes these old root cellars were very well hidden. This portion of the yard was pretty overgrown. There were so many thick bushes and gnarled tree stumps that there was no telling what was hidden beneath the runaway yard. Even when I did call the lawn people to come, I never asked him to do much around this side of the house. It was like a no man's land out here.

"Use your foot, Tamara. Help me! Feel around and see what you can find. It's got to be here. I know it is here. I know it like I know my own name." Chloe put her fingers in her ears and closed her eyes. I didn't know why she was doing that, but I kept my eyes peeled and did as she asked. I carefully walked around the abandoned portion of the yard and tapped spots with my feet. I didn't uncover anything unusual except some rotten tree limbs and a metal ring.

Metal ring? I waved my EMF detector over the metal,

and to my surprise, it responded. There was no electricity out here that I knew of. So, there was no reason for there to be a spike in the electromagnetic field in this spot. Perhaps there were some underground electrical lines.

"Chloe? I think this is what we're looking for—a ring. I found a door. Come, help me." I shoved the equipment in my backpack and tossed the bag to the side. Together we removed the limbs and debris that had stacked on top of the metal ring. It was connected to a wooden door. It looked like a trapdoor. It wasn't very large, and it was certainly very old. This had to be the root cellar Joey was talking about. I suddenly didn't know how wise it was to bring Chloe to a dark and gloomy cellar that was potentially home to an angry ghost who had the power to smack her around.

I didn't have an opportunity to ask her because she was on her knees, digging in my bag. She doused herself with my bug spray, tightened up her ponytail, and reached for her flashlight.

"We need to open it, Tamara. No backsies! I've got to get down there and get that clock. We need it, all of it. The clock, the book, and the box. They are definitely connected. You going to help me or what?" Chloe cracked her fingers as if she was about to step into a boxing ring and go ten rounds with someone.

Being the responsible adult that I was, I said, "I'm going first—end of subject. Let's see if we can get this door up. It looks pretty old. I wonder..."

As we reached for the metal ring to pull it up together, a big black bird passed overhead and cast a shadow over us. The thing flew so low I thought it would tear my hair out. I could almost see the color of its eyes. Black, just like the wings and the talons. I had never seen a bird like that before. It was too large to be a crow or a raven. I wasn't actually sure how big those birds got to be. I didn't really like birds too much. Anything that could fly and scratch your eyes out was not a friend of mine.

The bird let out a commanding screech, and I accompanied it with a yelp of my own. It was either trying to run us off or force us below ground. The last thing I wanted to do was stick around and find out. We tugged on the door, but it didn't immediately budge. It was so old it was wedged in there. Chloe picked up a stick and threw it at the bird. She didn't nail it, but the bird did swoop off to find a spot to glare at us from a nearby tree. I wasn't ready to call it a day yet. We had come too far, and we needed to find that clock. And get away from the freaky bird of death.

"We need a stick. A good stick. Stop throwing them away, Chloe! We need one we can use as a lever. Yes, that's it." I accepted a freshly found stick from Chloe's hand and slid it through the metal ring. She took one side and I took the other. The ring didn't want to cooperate, but the stick worked great. We lifted the door and dragged it away. How we planned on getting it back into place was another question. We couldn't leave an open cellar for some unsuspecting person to fall in. That had lawsuit written all over it.

A dank, musty smell greeted us. Whatever was down there promised to be bad and smelly. It didn't smell like death, not like a dead body or anything, but it smelled very old.

In the yawning darkness, I spotted a rickety ladder.

"Hand me that flashlight. I need to get a look around." Chloe offered me her ultra-bright LED light, and I did my best to get a good survey of the space. There wasn't much to see from my vantage point. I spotted some wooden shelves off to one side and a dirty floor. If we were going to discover what was in the cellar, we were going to have to do it in person.

I bit my lip as I waved the light over the ladder. All the nails appeared to be in place, and none of the ladder rungs were missing. The bird squalled at us again from the nearly leafless tree. I had a growing sense of urgency about this entire exploration. I didn't want to be in some hole in the ground after dark, especially if nobody knew where we were, but Joey. I guessed that he knew. I loved him, but he wasn't always reliable in an emergency. What was he going to do if we died? Welcome us to the afterlife?

"Please hand me my backpack before I lose my nerve. If we're ever going to do this, we have to do it now. Let me get down all the way before you come, okay?" Chloe nodded in response, a grateful smile on her face. Thank God she didn't argue with me about climbing into the spidery hole of death. At least there was that. I'd call that growth.

I hitched my backpack on my shoulders and secured it in the front with the snap. It'd been a very long time since I climbed into a hole like this. Lakefront Prison in Connecticut had an odd sort of hole in the ground. The warden put female prisoners in those lonely spaces when he wanted to punish them for misbehaving or not obeying orders. That whole place had a terrifying vibe. I didn't know why I was thinking about Lakefront Prison. *Focus, Tamara,* I told myself.

In that situation, the whole team had to climb down a ladder much like this one. I never forgot the feeling of being left in that hole for a full thirty minutes. The loneliness and the darkness were like being in a tomb. I swung my leg over the ladder, and my foot made contact with the first rung. I took a deep breath and gave Chloe a quick thumbs-up, then pressed on carefully. Chloe held the ladder just in case it decided to wobble on me. She didn't weigh as much as I did, and chances were if I made it down alive, she would too. *See, Tina Louise? I'm a great foster mom. Taking your daughter into hidey-holes in the yard, looking for cursed items and such.* I stepped down another rung, pausing only for a second to verify the ladder wasn't going to give way. With the flashlight in one hand, I made my way down the ladder slowly.

A deep feeling of loneliness came over me again. It was almost palpable. It hit me so hard it took my breath away and I expected to be pushed back. Whatever was down here made me extremely uncomfortable. As I began making my way down the final rung of the ladder, I called up to Chloe. "Come on down, but be careful on that third rung. It's a little loose." I watched her make the first few rungs down, and I waved the flashlight up to her so she could see.

"You are blinding me, Tamara. Cut that out!"

"Sorry! Just trying to help." I used the flashlight to examine the room for the first time as Chloe came to join me.

Yes, the loneliness. So very lonely. It's been a long time. A very long time. Don't leave. Don't go.

"Did you hear that?" I paused as I listened closely. Was I hearing things, or were these merely thoughts popping into my head? I wasn't a medium who communicated with the dead, but no doubt, these were not my thoughts. I glanced at Chloe, whose face was as blank and unreadable as ever. "Are you picking up on anything?"

"I didn't hear anything. Was it a voice? What did you hear?"

"Female voice. She said she was lonely."

"I don't doubt it. This place is creepy." Chloe began making her way to the shelves beside us. They were wooden and dust-covered. They were gray and almost empty except for a few abandoned items, an old container and a wooden bucket, like the kind you would use to draw water from a well.

Lonely. So very lonely. Sister...

"Tell me you hear that? I can't be the only one. Chloe? Are you listening to me? I think it's Annabel."

Chloe grabbed the flashlight and lit up the far corner of the cellar. "I swear I saw someone standing in the corner. Did you see it?"

"Nope, but let's break out the equipment and get some baseline readings. Let's use the EMF for pinning down spikes."

Stay with me, sister.

"Now that I heard," Chloe said as she crept back to me. "Sister? Did you hear that too?"

"Yep. That's the same voice too."

Stay with me, sister. Forever!

Even as I heard the voice and tried to listen more closely, I heard the scraping of wood and the clinking of metal. Chloe grabbed my hand and raced to the bottom of the ladder. I didn't fight her because I was swearing, out of fear or anger, I wasn't sure. By the time we made it to the top of the ladder, the door had slid into place.

Now you'll be here forever...

I felt Chloe sag beside me and her eyes were closing. I reached for my phone, but I couldn't pick up a signal. There was just a crackling sound and hissing, no dial tone at all. Cradling Chloe's head, I tapped her cheek gently and tried to wake her. She didn't move, but I could see her eyes darting behind her closed eyelids. She was alive, but something was happening. She was in some sort of trance.

I screamed for help.

14

ANNABEL

Feeling Pratt's hands on my skin sickened me. I couldn't say when he came into my room. I had not sensed him until I felt his touch. The room was dark and cold. It was dangerous falling asleep with a candle burning, but I wished this once I had lit one.

"Annabel, don't be startled." His bushy beard rubbed against my ear as his hand gently cupped my breast. Lying on my side, I kept still, pretending I had not heard him and that I was asleep. That did not deter Pratt. "It is only your husband. Once, you used to love my hands on your skin. Remember that, wife? I do. Perhaps it's not too late for us. Despite all that has passed between us, maybe it is not too late. Let us begin to love one another again, Annabel. I'm willing to forgive and forget everything, but I need you to come back to me."

I shook my head ever so slightly. "We can never go back," I whispered to him. How could I ever love Pratt as I had Simon? Even when I loved Pratt completely, I had not loved him as deeply. I had given my heart to Simon and consigned it to the grave to rest with him. I could not give him what I no longer possessed, but there was no point in explaining this to Pratt. He kissed me and laid his head on mine. "I loved you, Annabel. Once, I loved you. Won't you even try?" I couldn't help but tense under his grip.

There would be no pretending anymore. Slowly I turned toward him and stared up into his face. It was black and empty. No, that was only an illusion! The darkness shielded much of his features, but I could see enough of him to know his gaze was fixed firmly upon me. Despite his gentle handling of my breasts, he did not mean me well. Why else would he sneak into my room in the middle of the night other than to demand his marital liberties? I tried to sit up, but he prevented me from doing so by pressing the blanket around my body. I strained to look into his eyes, but the blackness did not allow me to see. Pratt's outline, though familiar, had no substance. He had no face!

There had been plenty of time for my eyes to adjust to the dark. Was I seeing another foul being?

"Shh...don't wake up the children," the Pratt creature hissed at me, and I regained my voice. I could not move, but I could certainly scream.

"Let go of me!" I shifted under the blanket, but there was no moving the black figure. He was going to have to smother me, but I would scream. Mitchell would come and help his mother, but what could a child do against such a being?

Was this my own husband or an evil spirit? To my surprise, a light tapping on the door broke the horrible spell, and the Pratt thing lifted himself from my bed as I scrambled to my feet. There was nowhere to go, but at least I would be standing upright if he came back to finish his dark work. Then I saw his eyes. They were bright with a strange red tint to them. He gave me the most savage of looks, then walked to the door and eased it open as if he were a true man.

My eyes fell on my sewing basket. Silver shears were poking out, and I reached for them as fast as a hungry rat reached for an easy meal.

"Mrs. Ridaught? I thought I heard a woman crying. Are you feeling well?" Daisy's blonde head appeared as the black figure moved past her and vanished into the dark hallway. What evil was this?

"Not very well at all, Daisy. Would you mind helping me with my hair? I'm so hot this evening, and it's just a mess." It was an easy lie. I wasted no time pulling her into my bedroom while keeping an eye out for the shadow that looked like Pratt.

"I'm not very good with complicated hairstyles, but I can certainly help you with your sleeping braid, Mrs. Ridaught." She glanced at me nervously and then toward the open door but made no mention of the shadow. "Mrs. Ridaught? Should I fetch your husband?" I kept the shears behind my back and clutched them so tightly I barely had feeling in my fingers. I closed the door while shaking my head fervently.

"Thank you, Daisy. That won't be necessary." There was evil in the air tonight that threatened to take me down with it. I sagged on the bed. As a precaution, I slid the shears under my pillow. Keeping them close comforted me, which seemed a ridiculous thought. Who had ever stabbed a shadow?

Daisy was struggling to light a candle to brighten the room, and I couldn't avoid the sob that caught in my throat. Forgetting her task, she came to my side. Daisy and I had never been true friends. She was a servant, and I was the mistress of this place.

Pratt swore I agreed to the hiring of a governess, but I couldn't recall any talk of anything like that. I had never had such a bad memory. It was entirely possible we had the conversation, but I wasn't sure. I wasn't going to push him on this issue. I was afraid that if I did, all my secrets would come pouring out. I don't know why I believed such a thing. If I let myself get too excited or too angry, I would tell him everything. About my dreams. About my dead sister, Betsy and my mother, both of whom watched me from various mirrors in the house.

"I heard you crying earlier, and never a more mournful sound have I heard. Mrs. Ridaught, why were you crying? I don't wish to pry, but I understand how difficult marriage can be. The people we love the most are often the ones who administer the most pain. I'm sorry for whatever sorrow you are experiencing. Please, feel free to talk to me. I am no gossip and am hungry for friendship."

Daisy's confession surprised me, so much so that I forgot about weeping. My curiosity stirred as I focused my attention on the young woman sitting beside me on my bed. My hand inched toward the pillow, and my fingers rubbed across the cold metal.

"Did you see the shadow, Daisy? He was here in my room. I think it wants to kill me!" I hadn't expected to make such a confession, but now that I had, I waited to hear her response. Perhaps my earlier observations of the young governess had been shortsighted. I could use a friend and a confidant.

"I heard you crying is why I came, Mrs. Ridaught. You were crying, and it broke my heart. Then as I approached the door, I heard you screaming. What has happened?"

Previously, I had considered Daisy a rival for Pratt's affections. She would've been if I had any interest in commandeering them again, but I did not. I hadn't thought about Daisy much before, but knowing Pratt had another object to worship besides me had brought me comfort.

"You saw nothing?"

She bit her lip and continued to deny seeing anything. "I only came because I heard you crying. That was you, wasn't it?"

"No, Daisy. That wasn't me. I woke to find a man in my room, but it was no man. It was a shadow, and it terrified me! Your knock on the door startled it. You saved me, Daisy!" I released the shears and embraced the governess with sincere thankfulness.

She hugged me back and then patted me as if she were comforting one of my children. Daisy smelled like flowers and herbs. I couldn't quite distinguish which flowers or what herbs they were that comforted me so.

"There now. We all have bad dreams, and sometimes they can seem very real. You are awake now, and I'm here. All is well." She held my hand, and I could see the delicate features of her pretty face perfectly.

"I was not dreaming. I was very much awake. It touched me." I shuddered at the memory of it all. Was I losing my mind? Was that my destiny? My poor Anita had certainly believed it was, and now she was gone.

To my surprise, Daisy kissed my cheek. It was innocent enough and yet caused me to flush in places I didn't expect. Daisy smiled, and I looked away. I wasn't sure how to respond to this uncomfortable but not unwelcome situation.

"I know firsthand men can be brutes. I am very sorry you are troubled by evil dreams. I know you and I haven't had much of a chance to talk, Mrs. Ridaught…"

Offering her a smile of my own, I said, "Please call me Annabel. Nobody calls me that anymore and I do miss it. I would very much like to be friends."

"It would be my pleasure, Annabel." All of the awkwardness of the kiss vanished as she released my hands and touched my hair. "Let me brush it out before I braid it. It is quite tangled. Look! The moon has decided to appear, and we will not need that candle after all. Where is your brush?" I told her, and obediently turned my back as Daisy retrieved the hairbrush from my vanity table. With skilled fingers, she began working the tangles out of my hair. Strangely enough, my fingers were eager to wrap themselves around the handles of my shears.

I didn't feel threatened by Daisy, but touching them comforted me. I decided then and there I would always keep a pair of shears near me. Never again would I be caught without them. I would also look through Anita's belongings. I still had a box of her amulets in my armoire. Maybe in the depths of her treasures, I would find some amulet to protect me from the shadow that pretended to be Pratt.

"He doesn't hurt me, not the way you might imagine. Pratt is not a cruel man. What did you mean when you said men were brutes? Have you been married before? You are so young, Daisy. You can't be more than twenty." Daisy's busy hands worked on my hair and I heard her sigh.

"I never married Annabel. Loren drowned in the pond behind his house before we took our marriage vows. I was two weeks away from being Mrs. Loren Wells. I shouldn't say this, and I don't expect you would understand, but I was rather relieved. I never wanted to be a wife. I never wanted to leave home." I kept silent as Daisy divided my hair into three sections and began weaving a tight braid.

I whimpered, and the younger woman apologized. "Your daughters complain about the same thing, Annabel. I can be too rough with a hairbrush. My apologies. It is easy to get lost in my thoughts when my fingers are enjoying such silky hair. My hair is a lively color, but it feels as itchy as a scouring pad. On rainy days arranging my hair is more like fighting a bramble bush. I swear it has a mind of its own, but your hair flows like water."

She tied the end of the braid with a bit of cloth I handed her. Slowly I turned to face her. It felt odd that a near-stranger was sitting so close to me on my bed.

"Nonsense, Daisy. You have lovely hair. You are beautiful, as you must know. You have eyes, and there are plenty of mirrors here. Why have you come to this lonely place? It is a long way from anything that should be of interest to a woman your age. Even if you never wanted to marry, there are other vocations besides being a wife."

"A governess is a vocation. There are far worse things to be, Annabel. Here, I can spend my time with the children. Although I admit, I am lonely for the company of adults at times. Children, I understand."

"I had a sister. Her name was Betsy. I miss her. Did you have sisters?"

Daisy smiled cryptically. "Many, but I'm afraid only a few of us survived. We had a hard winter, which took Nona. That spring, my oldest sister Elizabeth died from the cough. In some ways, you remind me of her. She was very lovely, too. From the moment I met you, I was stunned by your beauty, Annabel. Your daughters are pretty, but not quite as lovely as their mother. If you don't mind me saying, I think you are the most beautiful woman I have ever laid eyes on. Mr. Ridaught should take care to love and care for you, or some other will come and steal you away."

I caught my breath at her unexpected compliments. I wasn't quite sure what to make of the attention. How had she known I would need rescuing? I had not been crying earlier, so there was no reason for her to be lingering in the hallway. Despite her flattery, I could not help but suspect there was some deception afoot here. She was up to something, but I did not know what.

"This is a place of shadows, Daisy. You must know this. I am telling you the truth. A shadow came to me tonight and the other night in the study. Tell me. It is just the two of us now, the children aren't here, and neither is Mr. Ridaught."

Daisy drew back slightly, but I would not be deterred. Surely, I imagined these things. "What did you see in the window? The woman? Mitchell says he saw nothing, but I know that he did. I need to understand. Tell me what you saw, please, Daisy. I need to know that I am not losing my mind."

As I waited for her answer, the room darkened slightly. A cloud must have passed in front of the moon and blocked its brilliant light. The absence of luminosity created an unusual depth of blackness. I could only see the outline of Daisy, but her hand was in mine again. "Tell me, Daisy," I begged. I began to detect the subtle edges of odd shapes forming along the walls. The room suddenly felt very cold and not warm and comfortable at all.

"I thought he would fall. He was perched so precariously. It startled me. I will agree it can feel lonely here. With Mr. Ridaught behaving so distantly, I can imagine why. Come out with us tomorrow. The children and me. We will go outside and bask in the sun, maybe have a picnic. That's all you need, Annabel. You should leave this lonely, dusty place, at least for an afternoon."

Daisy continued to speak, but her language was garbled as if she were speaking to me from the other side of a wall. Over her shoulder, I could see a shadow building, a small one the size of a child. Like the shadowy being that assaulted me earlier, I could see no defined features, only the outline. She had long hair and a large bow in her hair. Or was it a hat? I was frozen with fear as the form of my dead sister began to manifest behind Daisy.

Sister? Is it really you?

The clock began ticking on the mantelpiece. Daisy's hands were in mine, and they were cold and icy. Her face was so close to me, I could see her mouth moving. Her empty mouth with no words coming forth. Was she laughing at me? The clock ticked louder. It was so loud I could hear nothing else, not even Daisy's strange language. I shot to my feet with the shears in my hand.

Daisy must have seen what I held in my hands because she was on her feet immediately. At that moment I wasn't sure what I should do. Betsy was moving toward Daisy now at full force, her shadowy hands stretched before her. My body vibrated with fear. Wild anxiety overwhelmed me, but the ticking continued.

Would it go on forever?

Suddenly, the Betsy shadow raced toward Daisy. Hoping to warn her, I screamed, but the sound erupted muffled and lost in the darkness.

"Move, Daisy!"

The clouds which had earlier cast the room in pitch-black slid away and allowed the moonlight to reclaim the space. Within the odd shifting of light and darkness, with the balance of good and evil, I could hear Daisy crying. She was pleading with me to stop. There was a long, jagged cut on her arm and blood all over the front of her thin, yellow nightdress. My own nightgown was awash with crimson. The shears slid out of my wet hand and landed on the floor with a clunk. The clock ceased ticking and all went quiet, but only for a moment.

"I am sorry. Daisy...I am so sorry. Betsy...she charged you, and I swung at her. I did not mean to hurt you. What happened? What did I do?" I could hear my voice perfectly now. There was no more odd distortion. I crawled toward her, but Daisy began to scream. She howled in agony as I reached for her. The bedroom door was flung open, and Pratt fell into the room. This time he was only wearing his nightshirt. Amie was behind him, and I heard the footsteps of my other two children in the hallway.

Daisy collapsed into Pratt's chest, her blood continued

to spew forth and stain his clothing too. She was bleeding profusely, and no doubt would die if left unattended.

I spotted the shears. They were not far away from me, but Pratt saw them and kicked them toward the door. My little Amie quietly reached down and picked them up with her pale fingers. Her dark eyes condemned me, and she glanced at her father. Pratt shoved Daisy and Amie out of the room and into the arms of one of the servants who had come to offer his aid.

My husband closed the bedroom door and reached for a nearby towel. It was one of my good towels. I had done the embroidery work myself. Now he would bloody my fine work. Before I could scold him for such a slight, he pressed the perfect white towel on my arm, dabbing gently at the blood.

Silence passed between us as he worked to find a single cut on my arms or hands. There were none. Tendrils of my hair slid out of my braid and stuck to my face. I didn't know what would happen next. Would I be arrested? Evicted from my own home? I could only hope, for it would be the only way I could escape this place of shadows.

My husband's patient wiping of my arms and his disheartening silence added to my ever-increasing anxiety. "I saw you, Pratt. You were not yourself. You were made of blackness. And just now, Daisy, she was not herself at all. Betsy came, and I think…if I had not stopped it, I think Betsy would have swallowed her up. Is that what's happening to me, Pratt? Am I being swallowed up? Are we all shadows?"

Pratt rolled the towel up and helped me to my feet. He

placed it in the bowl of water that rested on my vanity table. I wasn't sure what to do, where to go, or how to proceed. I imagined I could hear my children's footsteps outside the door, and Daisy cried loudly from her own room.

"The clock began ticking, Pratt. I couldn't hear what she said, and I did see Betsy." From my reflection in the mirror, I could see he had not erased all the evidence. There was plenty of blood left on my skin. Enough to convict me and surely someone would want to. He eased toward me, and I awkwardly fell on top of my twisted bedcovers. His face remained a mask I could not read. It had been this way for a very long time. Once I could see my future in those splendid dark eyes, but not tonight. Not anymore. I saw the end of everything. I did not need a bowl of water or a scrying mirror to see the truth.

"I loved you, Annabel. Even with all your ghosts." He waved a bloody finger at me and put his other hand on his hip. Pratt muffled a cry in the back of his hand and watched me intently. Once he collected himself, he continued. "You are mad, Annabel. You have been for a very long time. You will have to go. It's best for the children, for everyone. I told you before. I warned you. You welcome the ghosts, you always have. Now you will have to live with them, but not here."

"You are sending me away?" I sat up and pushed my bloodstained hair from my face. "I cannot leave my son. I will not, Pratt. You cannot keep me from my son."

Pratt touched my face with his rough fingers. Suddenly, his hand gripped my neck, and he clutched it as if I were a chicken. Would he wring my neck? That would be a better fate than being sent to a sanitarium where I would never see Mitchell again. He put his mouth close to my ear.

"I killed him, Annabel. I knew. I always knew. I killed him." With one last squeeze, he released me. I closed my eyes. Unsure what would happen next, no blows came. The door closed, and I heard the sliding of a chair. I was locked inside.

Pratt's intentions were clear. As I descended into a fiery cascade of screams and tears, I cursed him.

The clock began ticking again…

15

CHLOE

I woke up with my head in Tamara's lap. She was patting my cheek with her hand. The flashlight flickered off and on, creating a strange psychedelic effect. "Chloe? Thank God! You've been out for a while, and I couldn't get help. You're going to be all right."

I sat up and rubbed my forehead. Drained didn't begin to describe what I felt. There wasn't a word to describe any of this. "She jumped me, Aunt Tamara. That's what she was trying to do in the house, but she didn't get it right. She's learning and evolving. Annabel is strong. Have we found a way out yet?" I got up on my knees. My ponytail sagged, and I felt winded as if I'd run miles. I hated running. It wasn't just physical exhaustion, but spiritual, mental, and physical rolled into one.

An odd whizzing sound caught my attention. "We have a signal! That's my phone!" I dug around in my jacket and produced my phone. I could hardly believe it. Just as I tapped on the screen, the signal faded. I saw the bars dropped from four to zero. Aunt Tamara confirmed the same weirdness with her phone too. The whizzing continued.

"That's my K2!" She shed her backpack and began digging through it. We were no closer to escaping this spider-infested cellar of death, but we were onto something. There was definitely a disturbance in the EMF field because the lights were bouncing around. She flipped the switch, and the audio barked at us. "Over here! I think we have something. It's tracking."

I took a deep breath. The air smelled electric as if it were going to storm in this small space. "I never noticed that. Did you see that?" In the corner of the room where I swear, I searched earlier, there was a small wooden cask. It reminded me of a Halloween prop, the kind you would use if you were trying to decorate a room in a haunted pirate theme. Tucking my hair behind my ears, I squatted next to it and rapped on it with my knuckles. It was hollow, and there was something inside it.

Tamara's device confirmed that the energy we traced stopped in front of the cask. Annabel hadn't led us to this treasure. I got the feeling she hated that we were here. She hated that she was so weak since she jumped me. I was too, but I was alive. Dead energy didn't reproduce itself as quickly as living energy.

As my hands reached for the wooden cask, a loud boom shuddered above us. "Hello? Tamara? Chloe?" The curse breaker Angela had found us! Light pooled in a small circle beneath the ladder. I grabbed the wooden box, and together Tamara and I raced toward the opening.

"Yes! We are down here! The door closed behind us, and we're trapped in here!" Tamara's shaky voice startled me. I always just assumed that because she was older than me, she had this whole paranormal thing figured out. What a dumb idea. Who could predict all the crazy stuff that went on here? How did one prepare for any of it? I grabbed Tamara's hand and squeezed it. I had so much to tell her. This had been a terrifying experience, but I knew so much more about Annabel Loper Ridaught than I did before.

"We are coming up, Angela!" I called up the ladder to her. "Let's book it before she comes back. I don't think we're alone, and this ain't over. Not by a long shot."

To my surprise, Tamara grimaced and pulled out her phone. "I'm going to do a few photo bursts on my way out. You never know what I might capture. You go first." Without another word, Tamara began photographing the room. The flash of the digital camera app on her phone really brightened up the place. We could have used that if the flashlight died. I didn't enjoy this space at all.

Sister....

No! Go away!

I tucked the cask under my arm and went up the ladder. Not cautiously enough, though, as my foot slipped on the third rung. I caught myself with my elbow. "Take your time, sweetie. Take your time." Angela's pleasant voice echoed down to me as I closed my eyes and tried to get my bearings. I was shaken up more than I believed. As I came close to the top, I handed her my treasure, and she helped me climb through the hole. Tamara was right on my heels.

"How on earth did you find us, Angela? We didn't even know this was back here."

"Dumb luck and my Girl Scout training. How long were you down there?"

Tamara stared at her phone screen. "About an hour, but you know what they say. A second can feel like an eternity, and an eternity can race by in a few seconds. Or something like that. We couldn't get a good signal on the phone. Nobody knew we were down there, so the chances of us being found were slim. God, I'm thirsty. Let's go inside and get something to drink."

"Sounds good to me," I confessed as I glanced back at the open cellar. "Shouldn't we close that? Just in case? I'd hate for anyone else to get stuck down there."

Tamara agreed, and the three of us scooted the wooden door back in place. The metal ring clanged as the settling door kicked up another cloud of dust. "How on earth did you move that by yourself? We couldn't get it to budge."

Angela seemed puzzled. "It was heavy, but not so heavy I couldn't move it. I have no upper body strength to speak of, not at all. I'd say whatever led you down there wanted to keep you there. At least until you found that. I guess that's what we're looking for?"

Tamara and I exchanged a grim glance. "We haven't opened it yet, but from the sound of ticking, I would say yes." We strolled the rest of the way in silence. Every few feet, I glanced over my shoulder because I kept seeing movement. A piece of white cloth fluttered by at an odd angle, even though there was no wind to speak of. A gloomy cloud sailed over us far too quickly. At least the angry bird of death had left us. Why hadn't we at least taken a picture of the blasted thing? I would never forget it. I could probably draw a sketch of it if I tried.

Pepe greeted us with a barrage of yips and barks. The feisty little dog had left me a liquid present in the hallway. I could smell it from the back door. I deposited the wooden cask on the kitchen table and reminded Tamara not to take her eyes off of it. I wasn't keen on going back to that cellar to retrieve it. After I took care of the job, I put Pepe in his kennel and joined Tamara and Angela in the kitchen. Thankfully, Tamara had a glass of tea for me. I guzzled half of it before stopping to stare at the box we'd retrieved.

"How did you know where to find it?" Angela asked us as she politely sipped her tea. She'd barely taken her eyes off the cask. "You found it, didn't you?"

"I had a bead on it, but Tamara's equipment helped. I think it was a team effort. Should we break it open and see what's inside? We never got a chance to look at any of it before it disappeared." Tamara put her glass in the sink and began studying the item. It was an odd place to hide a clock, but it served a purpose, I guess. It had an old-fashioned clasp hinge that resisted opening at first. Once she wedged a butter knife beneath the lip, the box opened. The clock and tin were there, but the tiny book was missing.

Angela rose from her seat and stepped away from the table. Her eyes were on the clock, her hands lifted as if she would toss the table upside down. She didn't like this thing at all. I didn't either. Tamara and I followed suit.

"What is it?" I whispered as Angela closed her eyes and made some weird sign with her fingers. The horrid clock hadn't gotten any prettier, but the initial shock of that leering face had already worked its mojo on me. I wasn't shocked, just disgusted. "Angela?"

"It's a curse, all right. When you said clock, I should have put it together, but these are so rare. It's a strong bit of hoodoo magic, this. It's a shadow clock, and very unique, very powerful. So much so that I'm not comfortable sitting this close to it. No wonder you wanted to leave it behind and put some distance between you and it. Your instincts are not wrong, Tamara. You should trust yourself more."

"What is a shadow clock? How do they work?"

Angela stepped closer and put her ear near the timepiece. "It seems quiet, but that won't last. Look at the hands. It's almost midnight. It clearly has an agenda, and it's close to fulfillment."

"Like what kind of fulfillment? We'll be dead by midnight? I'll die before midnight? What's the agenda?" I asked with more anger and fear than I expected to hear in my own voice. When she didn't answer me right away, I buried my face in Tamara's shoulder. "I never wanted any of this. Not this house, not this curse. This is so unfair."

Tamara hugged me, and I clung to her for a moment as I wiped at my face.

"You could think of it that way, but I don't think that's the lesson here," Angela said thoughtfully. Her words didn't inspire me.

"What do you mean?"

"I mean, this all came to you because you are strong enough to break this curse. It's not by chance. It never is, trust me. I know that all too well. It's not an accident. You're strong, Chloe Carol. Strong enough to break this curse for good. And you won't be alone. You have two strong intuitives with you."

Tamara breathed a sigh of relief, but I wasn't sold yet. "Really? That's good news. What do we need to do? Tell us what the next step is, Angela."

"I thought a water cleansing would be a good place to start, but I think we are way beyond that. This clock is old, and it will start again. I don't know what its triggers are, but they are certainly tied to you, young lady. Wait, what's in the tin?"

I didn't wait for an answer to that question. I went to take a look at it myself. I shook it. There was definitely something inside it. I opened it and dumped the contents out on the table. None of us had words to describe what we were looking at. The tin contained tiny bones. Please don't let that be a kid's bones. Please, I prayed silently.

"There should be a book. You mentioned a book. Do you see it anywhere?" Angela questioned us as she warned us not to touch the bones. "It's not safe. Don't touch them, Chloe."

"I don't see the book, but it was with the clock and the tin when I found it in the floor of my room. Does this mean I'm screwed?" I was having a hard time fighting the feeling of hopelessness. It was like it had followed me from the cellar. It suddenly occurred to me that while this was all overwhelming, I was being influenced. These weren't actually my feelings at all.

Annabel!

"When I was in the cellar, I went into a trance. Tamara says I was unconscious, but I think I got jumped. Remember? I woke up telling you. Annabel Ridaught jumped me in the cellar, and I got to see her life, or at least a strange snippet of it. It's not the first time either."

"Go on, tell me everything," Angela said as she leaned against the kitchen counter. "You can put those back in the tin, Tamara, but don't touch them with your fingers."

"Don't worry," she said as she used a paper towel to move the bones back into the tin. After she finished, she moved the clock and the tin to the kitchen counter. The three of us settled back around the table. I didn't want to be there with the clock from hell, but I was afraid to turn my back on it, seeing as how it had a tendency to disappear.

I relayed everything to Angela and Tamara, leaving nothing out. From the weird flirtation with Daisy to Pratt's confession of murder. "Always, she saw shadows. Even when she was a kid. She really believed the things she experienced were real, but nobody believed her, except Anita. When she died there was no one to protect Annabel, not in a supernatural way."

Tamara scrolled through the pictures on her phone as I finished. "Look at this, y'all. I think I captured a face. Tell me what you see." She handed me her phone, and I studied the screen for a few seconds. It only took me that long to pick it out. It was faint, but there was a woman's face, her mouth opened in a silent scream.

"I think that's Anita. It must have been her who led us there, Tamara. She wanted us to find the clock. That would be right because she only ever wanted to protect Annabel. She really tried her best."

Angela leaned over my shoulder and pointed at the face. It was like a smoky mist, but the features were distinct. "That's a great bit of evidence. She might be the reason for the clock. It's possible that she tried capturing the curse."

"Capturing? How do you do that?" Tamara asked as she turned off the phone.

"If she knew hoodoo or voodoo, probably the latter in this case, she would know the width and breadth of her power. If she couldn't break the curse, she could capture it. Put if off for a spell, as they say. She used this clock to do it. The curse is restricted to the clock, but it's not a permanent fix. Anita meant for you to find it. Annabel didn't curse you. She just believed in it, which made it stronger and more potent."

Tamara tapped her fingers on the table. "This is interesting, but we're back to square one, except now we have the clock and that creepy tin. What's next?"

"Those bones were an add on. A seal-the-deal kind of thing. Probably the remnants of an animal sacrifice. Not human, at least. That would be beyond me, I'm afraid."

I breathed a sigh of relief.

"The animal has to go. No living creature should be here, and I can feel that your other roommate has vacated the premises. I have to be honest with you, that might be for good. Once we break the curse, it might be impossible for him to come back. Is that okay with you two?" Angela glanced at the two of us.

Tamara answered quickly. "That's not even a question. Chloe comes first, Angela. No matter what. Joey knows that." The curse breaker breathed a sigh of relief.

"I'll call Lynn and ask her to pick up Pepe. I'm sure Linda won't mind. She knows Lynn and likes her. She's Linda's back up dog sitter. That's all the living things beside us."

I reached for the house phone since my cell battery was nearly dead. Lynn agreed to pick him up, but of course, she had a hundred questions. "No time, Lynn. Wait, your dad isn't home, is he?"

"No. Pepe will be fine, and I'd like the company, but this isn't fair. I want to know what's going on with you, bestie."

"I swear I'll tell you everything, but not right now. Please, do me this favor?"

"On the way. Be there in ten." Lynn hung up, and I breathed a sigh of relief. On the way back to the table, I heard Tamara.

"I don't like this. There has to be another way."

Angela offered her pretty, sunny smile, but before she could say anything, the clock began to tick. The three of us watched in horror as the minute hand crept toward midnight.

"We literally have no time to waste. Help me gather my things, Tamara. I need a hand carrying in the bags. I'll have to convince you on the way."

I stood in the kitchen, staring at the clock as the pair exited. I got the feeling I was watching my life slip away from me. This might be the only one I ever had. There was no guarantee I would come back as a ghost.

Not everyone did, and I didn't want to be a ghost.

I wanted to live. The clock ticked louder and then it stopped. I breathed a sigh of relief.

Oh, yeah, I sure as hell wanted to live.

16

ANGELA

My worries for Chloe increased by the minute. Claude would not like this. He would remind me that curses *can* be unbreakable. He would reference one he encountered in the Outback and how his attempt to untangle the thing nearly cost him his life. Claude did like that story. He told it often enough, back when it mattered.

The truth of the matter was that the Ridaught curse was as close to permanent as any I had ever encountered. It was old, almost ancient. I suspected the curse had been placed by an even older ancestor of Chloe's than the one she suspected. If it had not been for Anita's intervention all those years ago, what must have been around a hundred and sixty years ago, Chloe would not be here today. She would have never been born and potentially not her mother either.

The curse had been contained within the clock by the voodoo practitioner. She had been strong, this Anita, and aware enough to know that she couldn't stop it, only slow it, but why? That's the question that needed to be answered. Why couldn't she vanquish it, for surely if she had enough power to contain the curse, she should have been able to break it?

I could almost hear Claude clucking his tongue at me. My dead lover lingered close, but I refused to openly acknowledge him. Bringing a dead person into a curse situation was the height of foolishness, as I told Tamara and Chloe earlier. He would only muddy the waters and confuse me, confuse everything. Curses weren't generally attractive to the dead. Dead energy had nothing to offer the ghosts. But this one was so old and strong it had almost become a living thing. It had its own consciousness, and it would never stop trying to achieve its singular purpose—end this family line. Kill them all.

It had become a shadow.

A thinking shadow with evil intent that could take on the image of whatever the target feared or loved. It would, however, always present itself in a twisted, shadowy way. For at its essence, it was shadow.

The curse had its own intellect and its own will. It wasn't at the mercy of the original curse caster. That person, a woman, had died long ago. The curse probably began as foolishly as most, with an unintended offense. Some magic workers crafted it and believed in its power, perhaps even cultivated it. The curse became strong when it was shared through fearful whispers and grew in strength amongst the women of the family until it had developed a consciousness.

Anita, the only woman in the past who stood up to it, tried to defeat the curse but failed. In the end, she could only contain it in the Shadow Clock. Only she couldn't stop the hands of time from moving forever. That was out of her power, but for the child she loved, Annabel, she did what she had to do.

"Here, take this one." I handed Tamara a black crocodile bag that contained various salts, oil mixtures, and spools of twine.

"Oof, Angela. What you got in here?" Tamara said as she struggled to lift the bag.

"A whole bunch of crucial items and a few other things. Black salt for one."

Tamara peered at me as she closed the trunk. Picking up the bag again, she headed back with a murmur of something or other. I carried the other bag. It was full of power items, one of which was some of Claude's ashes. I wondered what he would think about me using him in this curse-breaking. I wondered if I would tell him.

"I thought black salt was for keeping the dead out of your house or off your property." Tamara eyed me as we walked up the steps and into the house. "Kind of extra measures, don't you think?"

She was having second thoughts about her friend, Joey. It was an unhealthy attachment, I thought, but none of my business.

"Very good, Tamara. You do know your stuff, don't you? Yes, and it only takes a little. Advanced curses like the one we are dealing with here might need a black salt ritual to release and banish trapped spirits."

"Trapped spirits?" she asked as she dropped the crocodile bag on the table with a loud thud. I could hear another young girl's voice in the hallway. Chloe returned with a friend and introduced me to her. The teenager shook my hand, and I greeted Lynn pleasantly. I immediately wanted to wipe my hand on my shirt. She was definitely, and without a shadow of a doubt, cursed too. Only hers was a different kind of curse.

You cannot save everyone, Angela.

Stay back, Claude. I have black salt.

I expected an argument. Claude rarely vanished without a fight, but I heard nothing more from my pushy dead ex. I breathed a sigh of relief. After a few minutes of chit-chatting with the second teenager, we encouraged Lynn to leave so we could begin our work. She was curious and I knew she wanted to stay, but that was not a good idea for her or for Chloe. One curse was enough. Imagine having to deal with Chloe's curse with Lynn's piggybacking on it.

Yes, of course, Claude. I will help the girl. Her curse is an easy one to break. She could go do it herself if she just applied herself.

I did not actually hear Claude, but I could easily imagine what he would say to me. He had such sympathy for the accursed. He would be quite giddy about all this. Enough meandering, Angela, I thought. Stay focused on your task. There will be time for your own unhealthy attachment later. It's not as though Claude is going anywhere.

What was going to happen if the clock struck midnight? That was a question I had no answers for. If we were lucky, it would strike midnight and nothing would happen.

Maybe not to all of us.

I said nothing, even though it was the absolute truth. If we worked fast, we would break this curse. We must do our speedy work, as Claude used to tell me before he died. We were training, novices to all the power of curse work, and strangers in a new field. We had to learn the hard way. We had been cursed that first year. Cursed by his mother, and then later by his ex-wife, both witches from a dark coven, but both powerful women with an axe to grind.

I am sorry, Claude. Poor choice of words.

I heard nothing. I closed my eyes as I opened the bag. Sometimes closing my eyes helped me see the invisible, but Claude had heeded my earlier warning apparently. I could not sense him, or anyone in the house, besides the Reaper and us. He worked here, so I didn't think he'd interfere. This detail of Tamara's email intrigued me immensely. The idea of working with a supernaturate or at least encountering one excited me.

If he was a true Reaper, he would be eager to collect a soul. That was his job. He did not care where they went, as long as they were collected and properly processed. Strangely enough, I got the sense the Reaper used to be a man who liked processes and procedures. He liked doing things the way they should be done. As I reached deeper, the Reaper growled at me, and I left him alone on the second floor.

He hung out on the second floor. I felt he really wanted someone up there but had been denied thus far. Who did he want, the girl or the dead boy?

Souls are far too important to be left behind.

I take your point, Reaper. I will do my best to serve you one tonight, but not one of these living souls. Now leave me to my work.

Remember me, curse breaker.

"Oh, I am sure I will," I said as I opened the bag all the way. I began pulling smaller bags out and set them on the table. Chloe returned after saying goodbye to Pepe and Lynn. It was just the three of us here now, except for the Reaper. He was very excited.

I did my best to close him out, but Chloe didn't miss anything. "I see what's happening to you. I can sense the struggle. Is it always like that? Do you frequently smell electricity? Is it Joey? I can't feel him at all." She rubbed her arms as if she were trying to warm them.

"No, I don't smell anything, but sometimes I taste almonds. I think the variances amongst mediums are just the different ways our bodies process spiritual information. And no, it was not Joey I was speaking with. It's the Reaper. That's what you've named him, I believe. He doesn't mind it. The Reaper kind of likes that name. He's here to collect a soul. Let's deliver him one to keep him happy. You could very easily push him outside, but you'll never be able to get rid of him. He was assigned here by the higher-ups. This is his job. It's strange, though. I usually only see his kind at graveyards and cemeteries, not in a house."

Tamara froze when she heard me say that. "We don't want him taking anyone, Angela. If we can help someone pass through the light, that's what we'll do. Not turn them over to the Reaper."

"I feel I need to explain, so we are all on the same page. I need you to both understand this. Our goal tonight is to break the curse, not set people free or to determine where the dead go. That's largely out of our hands anyway. If we can, we will help, but the goal is to save Chloe from whatever destiny this curse wants to put on this young woman. It's not ticking at the moment, but who knows how long that will last? So happy thoughts, Chloe. Think happy thoughts."

"What?" she asked me as if I had two heads.

"Keep it positive. Your negativity, your loss of hope, your sorrow, that's what makes the clock tick. Think about someone you love, like a boyfriend."

Chloe's eyes widened, and Tamara whispered, "Bad choice, Angela. How about your Mom? She's someone you love."

"Yeah, but I'm sad because she's dead." We all three of us glanced at the clock. It wasn't moving.

"You love Joey and me. We're your family. I'm not dead. You can go to any college you want. You have your pick of which city you want to live in. When this is over, Clovie, we'll go anywhere you want. We don't have to stay here. We can go to the beach and live in a beach house. Whatever you want. I promise." Tamara's hopeful smile couldn't hide her glistening eyes. She really did love her foster daughter a great deal.

"Nobody calls me that except Mom. She used to call me Clovie. Nobody knew. How did you know?" Mission accomplished. Chloe was smiling big, with tears of joy for a change.

"I don't know," Tamara answered as she hugged the teenager as lovingly as any mother. "It just came to me. That's who you are, always. Now let's break this curse. How do we use this stuff, Angela?"

"We're going to start with the clock. Let's put it on the table. Chloe put this bag in your pocket. It's like a medicine ball. It has special protective amulets made for you specifically."

"Oh? Who made them?"

"Claude and me. They smell a bit, loaded with eucalyptus, camphor, and sage. Keep it on your person. It will sicken the entity hidden in the clock."

"Is Claude coming? I haven't met him yet. Is he a curse breaker too?" I didn't know what to say. It was my own fault having to answer questions I shouldn't have to answer. I could have avoided all this if I kept my mouth shut. "Claude had a big heart. He loved this kind of work," was all I said.

Chloe mumbled an apology and didn't ask anything else about him. I pushed him out of my mind too. "Okay, I think we're ready for that clock. I have a bag prepared, a big bag. This is a mixture of salts and oils. We're going to put the clock inside the bag and then…"

The clock began ticking, and I hurried to finish sealing the bag. I listened along with Chloe and Tamara. The noise stopped, but we were only one minute before midnight now. Whatever was going to happen was going to happen soon. I checked the seal on the bag, and it was good and set.

"Now what? How long will that last?" Tamara asked as she stood beside Chloe. The teenager was readjusting her ponytail. Her eyes had dark shadows beneath them. Too bad she couldn't rest first, but that wasn't possible.

"We have to go back. We have to find Annabel. She's the key."

"I thought you said Annabel wasn't the cause of the curse. Not the true curse caster," Tamara said unhappily.

"She's not, but she added to it. That book, the one that's missing, was hers and she has to give it back. That's the most recent binding. I'm sure it's a sloppy binding. I can't see her being a powerful priestess, not like Anita. We need the book. You have to go back, Chloe. I will go with you and watch from nearby. I will not be able to influence your ancestor. She is not my relative, but yours, but I can show you how to interact with her intentionally. She wants your help, or else she wouldn't be jumping you on a regular basis."

"Aunt Tamara, this could be the only way. The shadow clock could begin ticking any moment, and there is no more time. The bag of salt will keep the clock weak. Say you understand."

Tamara said honestly, "I understand, but I don't have to like it. What other things can we give her to help? Something besides medicine balls and good luck."

I laughed at that idea. "Oh, I think we can do more than that. In my pocket is a powerful stone, Chloe. It's called hematite. Now, this particular hematite is fused with onyx. It's both hard and resistant to negative energies, and in your spiritual travels, you will find that it will also push back those negative thoughts, the ones that aren't yours. Yeah, I know about them. Keep these in your hand, and she can't foist her feelings on you. This is an invaluable tool."

"What will Chloe do when she gets in there? To the past or whatever? Then what?"

I said in a calm voice, "Chloe needs to have a come-to-Jesus meeting with Annabel. She has to give up."

"Let's go. How do we do this?"

"Tamara, come sit with us. Right here on the floor of

the kitchen. I'm going to guide her into a soft meditation. It will only take a few seconds for us to cross over to the other side. Don't be frightened. We will simply go to sleep, but we are not sleeping, we'll be in the other world. The world of the dead."

"I don't guess there's a Plan B?"

"Not at all. Please, trust me. Trust us. Chloe is a natural medium. This isn't hard for her or me. Just be patient, and if that Shadow Clock begins ticking, pray."

Tamara didn't like that last sentence and I wasn't a big fan either, but it was the truth. "Let's do this, young lady. Lean back on the floor and lift your knees. There you go. Comfortable, see?"

The cold kitchen floor was anything but comfortable, but we wouldn't be here long. I could have brought Tamara with us, but she would be too worried about Chloe to be of any help. Best to keep that bit of information to myself and do the best I could with what I had.

This was all going to work out for the best. I could feel it.

The clock ticked once. Twice. Then it stopped.

"Chloe, take a deep breath in and release all your fear as you breathe out," I began in a soft, calm voice.

I was happy to see Tamara had joined us on the floor. "Again, only slower. Fill those lungs and slowly release. Focus on the blue light that is gathering around you…"

And then we were gone.

A woman walked toward us.

Tamara lay sleeping on the floor, or it appeared so to me since she had not crossed over. Chloe and I were awake and watching Annabel come straight for her. Annabel didn't see me. I glanced down to see my hands were invisible. There was only a faint trace of me here, but it would be enough to guide Chloe when needed.

I would have to risk using the clock. We would have to bring it out and put it in the light. The light would summon the curse so we could destroy it. At least, that was my hope and prayer.

So it began.

17

CHLOE

Annabel waited for me at the end of a long dark hallway. She was younger looking than I remembered seeing her. She'd been in her thirties at least, the night she unknowingly stabbed the governess. This time, she appeared dead, but not sickeningly so. She had skin, and her bones were not showing. I hated it when the dead presented themselves as rotting corpses. I never got used to it. Annabel's gray skin and the dark circles under her eyes saddened me. She had been a pretty woman at one time, and I knew that she'd loved, at least twice. She certainly cared for her little boy. As if she read my mind, a tear appeared in her eye.

"That's what she wants, Chloe. She wants your sympathy. It makes her stronger. This unfortunate picture is how she sees herself. The truth is probably far more disturbing."

Thank goodness you can hear me.

"Yes, I can hear you, but I won't come into your mind much. The less interaction she has with me, the happier she'll be, and I think she can hear your mind, too. She is your relative, and you do share abilities. Let her show you what she wants you to see, and then ask about the book. Be firm. She didn't escape the curse, but you can."

Got it.

Annabel walked closer. She wore a light blue dress. It had no sleeves, just a long skirt and a simple top. It was a modern interpretation of what she might have worn.

"She's reading your mind. She wants to relate to you."

As Annabel glided slowly toward me, I saw that her haggard appearance had improved. I didn't need the curse breaker to tell me what was happening. Annabel was "borrowing" my living energy to present this likeness for me. She was enjoying the use of my energy, but it would make me sick if I let it go on too long.

"Annabel, you know why I am here, don't you? I need your help. I have the Shadow Clock. It is still ticking. Did you know that? Did you try to hide the clock from me? Why?"

To my surprise, the tall girl put her finger to her lip and shushed me. She spun about in slow motion and waved for me to follow her. I did and found that I, too, was moving in slow motion. What was ahead? Were we still in the plantation?

With each passing second, I noticed something new about Annabel. She was quite familiar to me now. She now had a touch of pink in her lips and spiral curled hair. Her skin was becoming more lifelike and less ashy and gray. She could almost pass for my sister. The similarities between us were unbelievable.

Yes, sister. I need a sister. You see me! I cannot find you, Betsy!

"I am not Betsy. My name is Chloe."

A murderous wave of nausea clobbered me, and I bent over double in that cloudy hallway. The floor was uncertain, the walls impossible to detect. I felt faded and detached from Angela and my own body.

My Betsy.

She's trying to jump me or something, Angela! She wants to take over my body! Oh God! I think that's what she wants. She wants to be me! This is a trap. She didn't set the curse, but she's using it to kill me so she'll live again!

Angela's voice sounded weird like it was echoing from a distant chamber. I could only pick up a few words, and one was hematite. I remembered that I had it. I held it out to Annabel and shouted in a commanding voice, "Stop!"

Everything did stop, and we weren't moving anymore. We were still in the hallway. Annabel's transformation ceased too. Thankfully, she was no longer siphoning my energy. I clutched the beads tighter and showed them to her again. She frowned and crossed her arms. *Where exactly are you taking me?* Annabel stared at me, not with hate, but with curiosity. She wanted to hate me, but there was something about me that surprised her. Something she had not expected.

Where are you taking me?

You came back, Betsy. You came back, and you found me after all this time.

"My name is Chloe Carol, Annabel. I am not Betsy Loper." Before I could argue with her further, she offered me her hand. She raised an impatient eyebrow like an older sister would do to a younger. I can't say why, but I took it. It was warm, and I wasn't sick now. The nausea had passed. Annabel had moved on from trying to jump me. She had a serious expression on her face, not a frightful one. The haggard shadows from beneath her eyes had vanished, and she was her true self. Tall and pretty and very happy because she was with Betsy.

But I'm not Betsy!

"Let her believe it, Chloe. It cannot hurt anything. Let her see you as Betsy. She wants to show you something. Follow her. I am coming with you."

"Sister, I am here. What do you want to show me?" I said in my most honest voice. I wasn't comfortable with lying to Annabel, but this was the way it had to be, apparently.

Remember hiding from her? Hiding in the closet with the clock? Remember all the times we had to move the hands for her. She never loved us, Betsy. Why did you leave me? I have searched for you, Betsy. I searched everywhere. You left me alone. Alone with all those shadows. I was afraid. All my life, I was afraid. I waited for you in the closet, but you never came back.

"I am sorry, Annabel. I tried to find you, but it was black. All black," said another voice.

Betsy was right next to me. She was so small, not even six years old. She had long hair with a big bow positioned to the right. She wore a simple dress with a light blue pinafore. Strangely enough, she reminded me of Alice from Alice in Wonderland. She was a lovely little child.

There was a familiarity about her that I would not have believed. It wasn't just that she was familiar of face. She was someone I knew and knew well.

I squatted before her, and Annabel watched us patiently. She wore no expression except curiosity. It was then I noticed the cleft in Annabel's chin, so like mine. She hadn't had a cleft before. I was worried. Somewhere in the distance, I could hear the clock ticking.

Angela, do you hear it?

There was no answer. I was alone in this hallway of eternity, with one ghost who was working hard to steal my identity and with another that used to, in another life, be me. I had lived, and I had died.

Once I had been Betsy Loper. I had been the one meant to break the curse, but it was not to be. Mommy was sick, and I was sick, but we were different kinds of sick. I cried for Mommy and Anita, but Anita was with Mommy. I was dying, and I was so hot. Annabel was hiding in the closet with the clock. We could hear Mommy screaming, and we always hid when she screamed at poor Anita. Only I couldn't join her because I was dead.

I am dead, Annabel! Help me, Annabel!

But she didn't help me, she couldn't help me. I was a ghost now—a ghost who became a shadow and faded into nothing.

I became nothing.

Then I came back with a mission. The curse must be broken for all of us. I had a new Mommy. A good Mommy, but the curse worked on her mind too. I couldn't help her, either. Not the way I wanted to, not so that I could keep her. In this life, I had no sister.

The little girl stared at me with tearless eyes but looking into those eyes was like peering into sadness itself. "I can make it right, Betsy. You have to help me. You have to go with Annabel because she's so lonely. Annabel has to go with you, not me. She knows who I am, I do too now. We are one and the same, you and I, but Annabel belongs with you, Betsy. There is no Annabel for me in this life. Please forgive her for not finding you. Forgive her for not saving you. She was only a child. Will you help me? Help us?"

I was kneeling before Betsy. Her answer was a long, thoughtful hug. I wept as I had never wept before. As I held the child, the one I had once been in another lifetime, I saw all that should have happened for me.

My missed future swirled around me like a cloud, and in it I could see everything. With it all was Betsy's sadness. I would have gone to a girls' college. I would have married for love, and I would have loved my children completely. I would have sailed around the world and died doing what I loved, exploring the ruins of forgotten civilizations. I would have lived.

I stopped crying, and she took my hand. She—no, I— wanted to know what I was doing now. *I'll show you, Betsy. I am living, I swear!* I opened my mind to her. *I help the ghosts. We all see them, all the women in our family see the ghosts, Betsy. There's no need to be afraid of them. They only want us to help them so they can go to the happy place. So they can step into the light and find peace. I will teach the others, I promise. They will never suffer and wander in the shadows. I swear it. I am going to college, too. I want to build things, castles perhaps. I may or may not marry, but I will love deeply, and I will explore for us both. I promise.*

Please, help me remove the curse! Help me set us free!

Annabel was with us. I had not sensed her arrival, but she was here and watching. I wondered how much she could see. How much did she know? She hovered quietly near Betsy. Having found her, she would not want to let her go.

No, I will not let her go. She is my sister. My sister alone.

That's right, Annabel. She is yours alone. And you belong with her. Not in my time, not in my life. Please say you understand.

She placed a small book in my hand. The book that belonged to the clock!

"Thank you," I whispered as Annabel took Betsy's hand. I knew what I had to do for them. I would make the light, and they would leave the Ridaught Plantation forever. They would travel to a place of peace, far from this wretched in-between existence. The girls smiled at one another, having found each other at last. Having what she had truly wanted all along, forgiveness from her little sister, Annabel abandoned her plan to possess me.

It would have failed at any rate. Possession does not equal life, not in the slightest.

We only get one shot at this thing called life, and if we're lucky, we might get a second chance at making things right. This was one of those rare circumstances, and I decided to take full advantage of it. I closed my eyes and made the light. I made it warm and dull at first, so as not to scare them. Too much brilliance can excite and terrify the dead. I needn't have bothered. The sisters only had eyes for one another. They were all smiles. All transgressions had been forgiven. I didn't think about Annabel's children or her dead lover. This was the way it needed to be. Just like this, these two together. Forever.

As they faded from view, I found myself falling back into my body. We had accomplished it. To my great relief, I had brought the book back with me. I immediately gave it to Angela as Tamara held me close.

"You're okay. You're going to be all right, Chloe. I'm

here. I'm not going to leave you." The clock ticked away, but Angela did not stop to examine it. She read the incantations perfectly. Instead of strengthening the curse, she was weakening it, for after every passage, she rinsed her mouth out with salt water and spat in the sink. Fresh water flowed from the tap too.

After each incantation, she muttered the same phrase over and over again.

"This curse is null and void. You have no power anymore. This curse is null and void. Forever and ever."

The dishes in the cabinets began to rattle. I could hear the tell-tale sound of the brand-new chandelier swinging in the front room. The whole house sounded like a great big ship at sea, caught in a mighty wind that promised to capsize it. This was the curse, alive and well and fighting back.

A shifting in the atmosphere pulled me from one realm to another and back again. A deep scream erupted from my throat as a swirl of blackness surrounded me. The curse was manifesting like black bees spewed out of the depths of hell. A strange humming sound filled my ears, like tiny motors. Tiny engines of pain. They bumped me and threatened, and I wanted to swat them away, but I had no control over my body. It was like having sleep paralysis, but I was wide awake. I shook from head to toe as my body vibrated from the dark energy that twisted around me. The bees melted into one black, shiny mass, and a face emerged. It was the clock face with its devilish eyes and screaming mouth!

"You can't have me!" I found my voice and suddenly gained control of my body. I collapsed into a pile, but

Tamara was there, pulling me close to her. I could see this realm. The blackness remained, but it wasn't as close. It had faded a bit and was being pushed away by something I could not see.

I clung to Tamara as we crashed on the floor. Angela continued to turn the pages of the book. She screamed the incantations, repeated the salt gargle, almost choking a few times, and ended each passage with the declaration, "*This curse is null and void. You have no power anymore. This curse is null and void, forever and ever.*" Tamara and I began whispering it too. It was like a strange song, a round, with each of us saying the phrases in turn, but together. I envisioned a circle of light around me, around all of us, and then finally around my home.

The black twisting shadow began to moan, and then I heard whistling like a tornado was blowing past me. I knew firsthand what a tornado sounded like.

The wood in the house creaked and popped as if indeed a great storm were passing over, and the barometric pressure dropped to unprecedented lows like we were in the eye of the storm.

We continued to mutter the words and time felt as if it stood still. Angela collapsed in the kitchen chair and reached for the matches on the table. Her hands were shaking and she was drenched from head to foot.

"We have to burn this book! We can't risk it being found again, not by the living or the dead!"

Tamara got an ovenproof pot out of the cupboard and put it in the sink. "I will light her up and drop it in here."

"No! I want to do it! I promised Betsy I would do it." I got up and walked to the sink with the book in my hand.

The air was calmer, the floor was wet, and my ears popped. The clock ticked so loudly I could barely hear anything else. Despite everything, it only took one match to catch the book alight. It went up in a few seconds. I dropped it in the pan and made sure it burned to cinders. Nothing could be left, not a trace.

Your curse is null and void. You have no power anymore.

"What about the rest of it, Angela? Should we burn the clock and the bones? Do bones burn?" I hoped we could burn it all right now. Tears of joy filled my eyes. It was definitely working. I could feel the grip of the invisible, releasing me. I hadn't noticed how squeezed I felt until the hands of the curse began to let go of me. I would have died, if not for Angela Webster.

"We will bury those items in salt bags, and they will stay buried forever. I know just the place to take them." I had no idea what she was talking about, but my brain was so tired, and I was so thirsty. I just wanted this all to end.

All of it, forever.

"Hey, look at the clock!" Aunt Tamara shouted. I did, and I couldn't believe what I saw. The time was after midnight, and I was alive. Despite the heinous face, the leering expression of the black clock did not terrify me.

The curse was broken and I was still me—the me of now, not the me of yesterday. I was not Betsy, but Chloe Carol. Daughter of Tina Louise Ridaught. I was me, and I was alive.

"Good job, Clovie," Tamara said as we watched the fire turn to ashes.

"Good job to you, Aunt Tamara. Mom would have been proud of both of us. Oh!" I said as I heard something I'd never heard before…mom's laughter. She was moving freely about the house. I knew that laugh. I knew her joy!

Mom had returned, but it would be only for a moment. I'd done what needed to be done. She could go now and not worry over me. She could leave and rest in peace, at least until I came to her when my time had ended.

One day, Mom. I love you.

I love you, Clovie baby.

CHLOE

"Sorry, Kevin. With my investigation going on, I'm afraid I neglected the Rachel Burns case. If you wouldn't mind giving me a few more days, I believe I can make contact. Keep in mind, this isn't an exact science, and as you know, I've been through a lot recently. I'm feeling better, but I don't want to push myself. You understand, right?" I let Tamara's boyfriend in the house and waved goodbye to Linda who had picked up poor Pepe. It was a little strange that she didn't want to stick around and chitchat as she normally did. Linda appeared to have been crying all night. The bags under her eyes were puffy like giant marshmallows. Poor Linda and Pepe. I felt sorry for both of them. I never got the chance to take the dog for a long walk or play with him like I had planned to do, but there would be other times.

Maybe. I wasn't sure. I might be leaving soon.

"Of course, I understand. I wouldn't want to put you in harm's way, not for anything. I don't object to waiting, but look at what I have." He waved a key in front of me. "It practically took an Act of Congress to get this, and I only have it for a day."

"Is that a house key? It looks old." Then it dawned on me: it was the key to the Burns Ranch. "Get out of here. Is that it? Seriously? How did you get that? Do you know how much the teens around here would pay to get a copy of this?" I joked as I snatched it from his hand. "Oh my gosh. I don't feel anything. This isn't the original. It looks too new."

"You're joking, right? You can pick up things from keys?"

I rolled my eyes and said, "Gee, you are stupid. I'm not a bloodhound, but yeah, there are times when I pick up things if I handle objects. It's hit or miss." He shrugged that off and peeked in the living room. "Tamara around? I saw the new car outside. It's a nice one. Did you pick that one out?"

"First question, yes, Tamara is around, but she's working on her book in her office. You know that's a no-go zone. She's on a roll, too. She's been in there for hours. You're taking your life in your hands if you interrupt the flow. Best to wait until she's taking one of her scheduled breaks. Next one is around 4 p.m." I tapped on my watch. "You'll have to wait a few more hours. Second question, no. I didn't pick her car out. That was all Tamara. I would never choose such a small vehicle or a red paint job. I prefer black. Shiny, glossy black. My car will be delivered tomorrow. They didn't have the one I wanted in stock and had to send out for it." I grinned victoriously at him, still clutching the key. I stroked it with my fingers like it was a lamp and a genie would emerge.

Kevin glanced down the hall like I was lying to him about Tamara. Did he think I would do such a thing? I liked the Kamara. No, the Tevin. What did Lynn call them? I wasn't good with couple name amalgamations. I was their number one fan. Seeing Aunt Tamara happy made me happy, and their relationship inspired me to continue believing in love.

All kinds of love. Like that goofy old song Tamara played when she was in one of her hippie moods.

Light of the world shine on me...love is the answer...

"What did you go with? An SUV? A black one, like the kind a SWAT team would drive?"

Together we walked into the kitchen, and I glanced over my shoulder to give him a thumbs-up. "I'm not sure what you mean, but yes. I chose a small SUV. Lynn and I are going to do some camping this summer, and it will pull a small pop up tent or some other gear. Good guess. How did you know?" I offered him a glass of tea as it was evident Kevin wasn't going anywhere. Did he plan on hanging around until Tamara finished? That wouldn't be for another few hours, although truthfully, I was sure she'd be coming out for coffee soon. Tamara liked working by half-hours. My job was to help her stay focused. With Kevin here, that would be impossible.

As it stood now, Tamara was mired in a bit of tricky research. She was stuck so deeply that she often got off track and failed to actually do the writing. Tamara was definitely a researcher at heart. She and the librarian were big buddies now. She called the house at least once a week to let Tamara know a special book had come in for her. It was good to have friends. Maybe I should do a better job of cultivating a few more.

It was Kevin's turn to shake his head like I was stupid. "Your aunt told me about the vehicle. I'm not a psychic, nor do I have any special powers. I'm not like you and Tamara, a paranormal person. I mean clearly, I respect paranormal people, but I don't have any of those abilities. I don't think. What you think?"

I tilted my head as I pondered his question. "Are you asking me if you are a medium? Do you know something I don't? Are you having experiences, Kevin?"

"I'm not sure. Forget what I said. I'm just talking out loud."

Tamara emerged from her office, her blonde hair piled up on top of her head. She was using her reading glasses as a headband again. She'd have them stretched out soon and would have to go back to the store to grab another pair. "I thought I heard voices. When did you get here?"

"I just got here. I'm sorry to interrupt. Chloe was just telling me that you are in the middle of a brainstorm."

With a snort of exasperation, she said, "More like a brain...something else inappropriate that I probably shouldn't talk about."

"Fart, Tamara. Brain fart. Ladies can say fart."

"Fine. Then that. I thought I was on the right track, but things have gone south. I need a break. Just for a few minutes," she said as she waved her finger at me. Like I was the drill sergeant. Tamara was the one who asked me to keep her on track. Had she forgotten already? Apparently so because she was out of her office and not writing a word. If she wanted to procrastinate with Kevin, who was I to say otherwise?

"Since you're looking for creative ways to avoid work, why don't you come with us? We're going over to the Burns place. I was thinking of a walk-through, just to see what I can pick up. There's plenty of daylight, and I'd like to take a good look. I'm assuming there is no power over there. No lights?"

"That's a great question. I don't know. Getting over there quickly before the sun goes down does make sense. Remember, nobody knows we have the key, except Mrs. Burns. The sheriff doesn't even know what I'm doing, and he wants me to solve this case. The weird thing is, and I don't want to give too much away, we just got some information on our tip line. Some things we didn't know before have come to light and… That's probably all I should say. I know you prefer to work without a lot of backstory. What do you say, Tamara? Do you want to go with us? Hold my hand while Chloe makes contact with the other side?"

Both of us made a face at him. He'd been with us too long to joke around like that. I didn't want to come off as a stick in the mud, but surely, I deserved a little more respect.

"I'm not kidding. The whole idea of going over there, I've been having…I've got apprehensions about it. I really want to see justice happen for this young woman. I was kind of hoping since she passed away so close to the Dead House she might migrate over here and seek help. That hasn't happened, has it?"

"It's been quiet since the curse breaker left. Except for

Joey, but he's not going anywhere. I haven't seen anyone, not even the Reaper. How about you, Tamara?"

"Not a soul. You know what, I could use a break. Let me get out of these yoga pants and grab my gear. Give me two minutes!" She kissed Kevin's cheek as she raced down the hall to her bedroom.

"We might as well hang out. You know her two minutes really means ten."

"I'm okay with that. I guess you heard about Lynn's father? He's going to do some serious time. I knew the law would catch up with him eventually. That whole family seems to have a death wish. I'm glad that Lynn has you. You're a good influence on her. She's more of a follower while you are a born leader. Any idea on what her plans are? Any luck on finding her mother?"

I shook my head. "Tamara and I talked about it, and she's agreed to allow Lynn to move in here." Obviously, Joey was eavesdropping because I heard him squeak on the staircase. It must've been the first he'd heard about the official ruling. I knew firsthand he didn't like this idea at all. He had been pretty vocal about it until he decided to pout and vanish. Classic Joey.

Kevin glanced around the corner, but he didn't go up the stairs. He knew about Joey, but he never talked about him openly. I guess the thought of your girlfriend living in a house with a dead male would be troublesome. From time to time, I got the idea that he didn't quite approve, but then again, he never said much to me about it. To my surprise, Tamara's two minutes actually meant two minutes. She had her backpack on her shoulder and smiled at us sunnily.

"This is just what I needed. A break from the keyboard and monitor. Nothing like some real-life experience to give me the goosebumps I need to pick up the plotline and run with it. You say you have some new tips on potential leads in the case? That's got to be exciting for you and the sheriff, not to mention the family. Does Rachel Burns' mother approve of what we are doing, or is this whole thing on the down-low?"

I climbed into the back seat of Kevin's pickup truck and bent my head around to glance at Tamara. "What? Do I use the phraseology wrong?" she asked.

"I guess technically not. I'm going to put in my head-phones so I can chill out. How long will it take to get there? I don't think there is an access road from the highway, is there?" I glanced up at the sky to check for clouds. It was a beautiful day, but when I had stepped out to get the mail earlier, I thought I smelled rain. I was ready for a good old rain. I could get lost watching the rain. I had a feeling that privacy was going to be hard to come by after this weekend.

Lynn was getting her affairs in order, and I would be helping her pack up her house. Most of her family's belongings, scant though they may be, would go into stor-age. The rest of her stuff would come here. I was both looking forward to it and also a little anxious. I really liked my solitude. That was the whole reason I picked a room on the second floor. Now Joey was living up there, and soon Lynn would be. Well, I would make the most of it. Such is life. I closed my eyes as I poked the earbuds into my ears. Without even looking, I tapped on the screen, and the music began to play. Wordless, instrumental music. The kind one used during meditation or preparing to go to sleep. I breathed in, held my breath, and then released the air quietly. I remembered my posture and made sure my hands were resting comfortably in my lap. It didn't take long to connect with the Burns property.

She knew we were coming, and she was as desperate as any dead person I had ever met. Then she was gone. The drive went quicker than I expected. I was hoping for a little more quiet time, but as Joey likes to say, it was what it was. I was more than ready for this. Coming here to look for clues about the murder was easy compared to what I had been through recently. That reminded me that I needed to call Angela when I got back to the house. I had a message for her, and I was pretty sure she wasn't going to like it. Angela's dead relatives were not happy about her current existence, and they were not going to allow her to continue harming herself.

Claude had to go. She wouldn't like the message, but it was a conversation we were going to have. What she chose to do with the message was on her. I couldn't decide her life, but I could be a good friend and a good person, just like she'd been for me. I would offer my gifts to her, offer to move Claude on and encourage her to encourage him to do just that, but it was her decision.

I opened my mind as we eased into the driveway. There were potholes aplenty, but it was a short trip. The Burns place wasn't nearly as large as ours. It was a rambling ranch-style home that had been neglected over the years. I didn't want to say this, and I sure wasn't going to confess it, but I'd been here before with a few teenagers. I didn't go into the house. Nobody did, but they liked to sit outside smoking weed or kissing.

I had known then that it was a haunted place. Not merely because of the story of the murdered actress, but because of the odd things that hung in the trees that surrounded it. I could see them clearly, but nobody else did. I was completely fascinated.

There weren't too many of the old trees anymore, but there used to be an oak grove here. The branches had been full of dream catchers. This land had been connected to ours once upon a time. These places were so haunted. I closed my eyes and opened them again. Sometimes it helps my mind reach into other time periods. I didn't need to go very far back into history. Although now that I'd seen the grove of dream catchers, I would no doubt be investigating this place on my own. Whether on foot or by car, I didn't care. It was going to happen

Kevin parked the vehicle, and we quietly stepped onto the property. Some time ago, probably back in the fall, a man had been here working in the yard. He had been frightened by what he saw. I could see exactly what he had witnessed.

A tangle of black, black lines was swirling in one spot. It was almost as if someone had taken a marker and colored in the air, only the marker smudge had a life of its own.

Inside the house, it would be much worse. I closed my eyes to control my breathing for a moment. I had to watch myself. If I allowed my imagination to run wild, anxiety would overwhelm me. I had to practice even breathing and continue to do the job I was meant to do.

This was my purpose.

Time to help the dead.

I walked up the porch steps and removed the key from my pocket, slid it into the door, and turned the lock over. Glancing over my shoulder, I gave them both an even look. I told them what I knew already.

"Don't touch anything, don't move anything. She wants to show us, but it's much worse. Worse than you know." That was all I knew so far, but it was going to get much worse. That's what she kept telling me, and I believed her.

Show me, Rachel.

19

CHLOE

The lights were off, but it wasn't dark inside. There were some blinds missing, and light poured through the dirty windows. I got the feeling that Rachel—I was assuming it was Rachel—liked it that way.

She didn't want anyone else here ever. She wanted life to remain as it was when she lived here. Her name was Rachel Gail.

Okay, Rachel. What do you want to show me?

Tamara was unzipping her backpack, and I could sense the spirit edging away from us. Others had come in before with their devices and cameras. She hated the cameras more than anything. They had invaded her life too much, both when she was alive and now in her death. They even took pictures of her as she lay in her death state. She was really mad about that.

"Don't. Put that stuff away. She's here, and she is really sensitive about it. We don't need it anyway." Tamara cinched the bag back up with an odd glance around the room. Kevin stood behind us, but he wasn't going far. I put his earlier question in the back of my mind. I would certainly follow up with him. If he was experiencing something from hanging out with us, I wanted to know about it. I was sure Tamara would want to know too. We were in this together.

"I'm sorry. I didn't mean to offend anyone. I'm putting everything away." Tamara's soft voice echoed in the near-empty space. What was once a plush living room now appeared more like a junkie's hideaway. There were empty soda cans on the ground, trash in the corners, and some broken furniture.

"Rachel. My name is Chloe. I can hear you and see you. These are my friends Tamara and Kevin. Kevin is a police officer, a deputy. He wants to help you. We all do." Rachel growled, but it wasn't meant to be menacing, not in any real way. It was more of a warning, like, "I don't trust you. Please leave me alone, or I will hurt you!"

"Rachel. You don't have to run from me. Show me the black marks. Show me where the things happened." Even as I spoke the words, I understood them. Rachel had made those marks. Each one represented a sin, a crime. The black marks were markers meant to be reminders to everyone that she had been a victim. Despite her success on the screen and her popularity in the media, Rachel had been a victim—a functioning yet tragic victim. In the end, just when she thought she'd left it all behind and she could overcome it, he took her down.

For the last time.

"I'm just going to run with what I feel because Rachel is not interested in having a conversation. I get why, but she is really damaged, and if we do much more than hang out here, it's going to be bad." I nodded at my investigative partners and hoped they agreed with me without much argument.

"Whatever you think is best. I'm just here to listen," Kevin said as he hung back a little. "I'm not trying to bust anyone or cause a problem. I'm very sorry we couldn't help this young lady when she was alive. This whole community let her down. I'm sorry, Rachel Burns. I'm sorry about what happened to you."

There was a shiver in the atmosphere. Movement in the ambiance here disturbed me. Rachel wasn't running from us — she was running from her killer! Tamara touched my shoulder softly. It didn't spook me, but it did ground me. I was grateful for the thoughtful touch.

"He is here, whoever killed her. There were two of them. One of them is dead. He thinks he's got the upper hand. He dominated Rachel's life and is doing it again, but there were two of them. The other one, he needs to be punished. She was on self-destruct. Everybody knew it. Everyone knew Rachel was going down in flames, and what did they do? They threw gasoline on her. She was their meal ticket, but they also hated her. She provided them with everything, and they couldn't stand her. He had always hated her because of her father."

Tamara whispered something, but I ignored her and kept going. She must've been talking to Kevin. I kept my eyes closed. Sometimes when I stepped into a busy environment, when there was a lot of spiritual activity happening, I could close my eyes and see the other world better. I was glad today was one of those days.

"Could you tell me more? Why did he hate her father?"

That was Kevin's voice now. I opened my eyes and saw black marks. Fresh ones. Rachel had returned, and she was drawing. She'd liked to draw, even when she was a child. If we search this place hard enough, we would turn up pictures and artwork. Her mother still had some. She loved her mother. Her mother loved her, but she was blind to everything that happened then and now.

"She says that's not right. He didn't hate her father. He hated her because of her father. I'm not even sure he knew who her father was, but in this man's mind, he felt threatened. Rachel was the epitome of success, and he felt as if she didn't give him enough credit. Oh yeah. He's a monster. I feel that he's here, but not all the time. He comes and goes, but he prefers it when it's dark. He doesn't like anyone to see who he really is or what he does. He hurt her. I think physically, mentally, and verbally. I think he would've liked it to be other ways too if you get my drift, but she was too smart for that. Things turned around, and he couldn't do what he really wanted to do. She got discovered, and the spotlight chased him away. That hurt her. The way he felt about her really hurt."

Tamara asked softly, "What does he look like? Can Rachel tell us what he looks like? Even if she can't tell us his name, a description would help."

Rachel was suddenly next to me and whispering in my ear. She said one word. "Carmichael. That's what I get. She says everybody knew him."

"That was her stepfather. His middle name. That's what the family called him. Everett Burns. Everett Carmichael Burns. Wow. You're right, Chloe. He's dead. He died of a heart attack a few years ago. Sonofabitch! I knew he was good for it!"

I put my hand out to remind him that we were not alone. The dead were listening. I was a medium, and this was a haunted location. Once upon a time, many dream catchers had gathered here. The energy of what they had done remained in this place, and a big part of what happened on my property was because of this one, both good things and bad things.

"She says there were two of them. Carmichael did this, but the other one knew about it. He came and looked at her. He saw what happened, but he didn't do anything, and he left her there bleeding. First, she was here, and then they took her out there." I could see Rachel's body broken and bleeding on the floor. "He hit her hard and suddenly. She was high when it happened, really high. The drugs had given her a false sense of security. They made her feel empowered and unstoppable. Because of her altered state, she believed she could take him on and that she could take them down. When he challenged her and came after her for more money, more everything, she let him have it. And with both barrels." I wrung my hands as Rachel got closer. She was so close that I picked up on the remnants of her drug use. "You have to back away. I'm sorry, but you cannot connect with me like that. That's not cool. Back off a little."

Tamara's hand was on my shoulder again, grounding me and strengthening me. Rachel whined briefly but did as I asked. She connected with me deeply enough to know that my intentions were good, but that was not an excuse for her to impart her illness to me. I didn't need that kind of problem. I'd been reading recently that addictions could be transferred. No, thank you. She walked into the kitchen and waved us through. Apparently, the tour was just beginning. I'd been wrong. Rachel was eager to tell us everything.

Can you get me out of here? He's coming. I know he'll come. He won't let me leave.

"Yes, I'll help you. That's what I do. I help people who want to move into the light. Is that what you want? Do you want to move into the light, Rachel?"

I'm not dead! I'm not!

"Shoot! This isn't going to be as easy as I hoped. She's confused. Really confused. One minute she knows she's gone, and the next she doesn't."

Tamara made a comment that made a lot of sense. "If she died under the influence of some type of drug, that can happen. I've seen it before. Just be patient and keep talking. We're not going anywhere. You want me to try? Just to give you a minute?"

I nodded as I struggled with mastering my emotions. It was getting thick in here. I twisted my neck, hoping the pain that had suddenly appeared would disappear. I did not like this feeling one bit. Whatever was happening here needed to stop. I wanted to help, but I didn't want to leave in a wheelchair.

"Hi, Rachel. Chloe introduced me, but in case you forgot, my name is Tamara. This is Kevin. We're friends, your friends. Rachel, can you show us your room? Is it back here to the left or to the right?" I didn't hear her voice, but I instantly knew the answer.

"She says to the right. Last door on the right. We can

come if we want to. She likes us. That's what she says, but she is afraid. I get this feeling of anxiety, and it's much stronger than what I normally feel from the dead. This is like intense fear on steroids. I think he comes back here on a regular basis, and she knows it. She is afraid not just for her but for us. We need to wrap this up." I glanced at Kevin in my attempt to express my concern.

"Ten more minutes. That's all we have. I promised Mrs. Burns we would only be here a few minutes. Help us, Rachel. Show us what you want us to see. Tell us who else was there." Kevin's voice echoed down the empty hallway. Man, local law enforcement has not done a good job of keeping people out. I could see that bothered him. His jaw popped as he examined the disturbed environment. How would they ever come back and gather evidence if this place wasn't secure? We needed a home run for Rachel to put this one in the bag. To bring this one home for her. Why all the baseball talk?

As we stepped into her room, I caught a strange feeling of familiarity. It was kind of like what I had experienced when I stepped back in time with Annabel. That experience had been far too immersive, and I knew better than to allow myself to go that deep.

"She likes playing baseball. For a little while, she liked Carmichael, but then there were rumors going around that her father was coming back. He wanted to see her, and that enraged Carmichael. Something happened to him and she knew it, but she couldn't do anything. She was a kid. This room was her sanctuary. For some reason, he didn't bother her when she was in here. Rachel was good with booby-traps. She got the feeling after the event that occurred with her father, the rumors of his return… she knew she needed to protect herself. You are one smart cookie, Rachel. They didn't give you enough credit for that, but you are one smart girl. She nailed her own window shut and slid a chair under the door at night to make sure no one came in. For further precautions, she left jacks on the floor. She never went to the bathroom after bed and never had sleepovers."

I paced the empty room and looked for black squiggles. There were none in this room. She loved this place. This is where it needed to happen. She needed to move on because Rachel Burns deserved peace. In this space, it could happen.

"Kevin, can you stand in the doorway, but outside? It needs to be just us girls in here. I'm going to talk with her and try to get her to see the light. Tamara, will you help me? I need you to focus your energy on me. It is going to take a little to break through to her, but I think we can do it. She appears to be experiencing a moment of clarity." Tamara agreed, and together we stood in the center of the room. Rachel was standing with us. For once, she wasn't all over the place. She wasn't scribbling or crying or wringing her hands or whining. In fact, she'd gone back a little bit. She was a little girl on the baseball field. If I had to guess her age, the one she was projecting was about seven.

"Rachel, I need to tell you something, but I don't want you to panic. I want you to stay just like you are. Just like you were before you stepped out on that field. Remember how you used to love to throw that curveball? How it made you feel when you could trick the batter? Confident and happy? That's what I want you to be, but listen. Okay?" The little girl between us looked up at me and nodded her head. Her blonde hair was pulled into pigtails, and she'd even taken the trouble of wearing her baseball uniform. She was happy at this moment. Not high, not scatterbrained. Not performing for the crowd. Rachel was her own self and peaceful.

But she couldn't stay in this room forever. Her tricks would not work forever. He was getting stronger and looking for ways to get in. The more people came, the more they came looking for her and summoning her, the harder it would be for her to leave.

Rachel was reading my mind, picking up on what I was telling her without me speaking a word. Her head and shoulders sagged as she sobbed. I didn't stop her. She'd been murdered. If anyone had a reason to sob, it was her. Maybe this was the way to do it. Saying it out loud wasn't as effective. Rachel had been a spiritual person in life and continued to be one in death. She understood the language of quiet.

Rachel, it's not your fault. Nobody's punishing you or blaming you. It was his fault. Carmichael did this to you, and he had help. Who was it? Who did this? Who else was there?

Lee. My brother Lee!

I kept that bit of information to myself for now. I would share it with Kevin and Tamara once we left the building, but I couldn't get that conversation started now. I had bigger fish to fry.

Rachel, if you stay here, he will find a way in. You have been so brave and so strong for a very long time. I know this was not what you wanted, and this is not what you deserved, no matter what you think, no matter what your faith. You didn't deserve this, Rachel. I want to show you something. I need you to trust me. I want to show you the light. See? I can make the light. It's safe. It's like this room, only he will never be able to get in there. I can promise you that. I want you to get closer to it. It's in the shape of a circle, and it is right in front of you. It's soft and yellow like a lightning bug. See it pulsating? It's warm and inviting, and you are welcome. Step through to the light, Rachel. Step through and find peace. Step through and don't return. Do not come back no matter what. You have to stay there because you deserve peace.

With a quick flick of her fingers, just like when she tossed a curveball, Rachel walked into the light and vanished.

I wanted to cry tears of joy. I wanted to celebrate her life and I would, but this wasn't over yet.

"Back to the living room! She's gone, but you knew that, didn't you?" It wasn't Tamara I was talking to but Kevin. I caught him rubbing his eyes with the back of his hand. This man was a sensitive just like Tamara and me. We were very different in our abilities, and he was just getting in tune with his, but oh, my gosh!

Tamara's surprised expression made me smile. "Hurry up now. This is really going to blow your socks off!" I didn't look back. I'd achieved what I wanted, and it had happened really quickly. In a negative sense, all of the people breaking into this place and communicating with Rachel had fueled the fire and enhanced her suffering, but it had also made her more aware of the real deal, and I think on some level she had been waiting for us.

Now it was time to deal with this joker.

"Most of the time, he hangs out in the dark squiggles,

the marker spots. I think she was trying to capture him, or maybe she wanted to record and remember his offenses. He wasn't repentant. He liked what he did to her. The only thing he regretted was not doing everything he'd intended to do. You know what? I don't want to wait for him to come in here. Let's go where he is."

"You lead the way. We will follow you." The three of us hurried out to the yard, pausing only long enough to lock the front door. I don't know how I came up with this plan, but I knew what I wanted to do. I knew who I needed to call to make it happen.

"Carmichael!" I stood in front of the smudge spot. Even though Tamara and Kevin couldn't see it like I could, I knew they could feel it. It was hard not to sense that kind of hatred and malevolence. After a few more years of roaming this property and tormenting Rachel, I had no doubt he would have had the ability to become something else. I shivered at that thought.

Well, that ain't gonna happen!

"Carmichael! I know you're there. I can see you, and I know what you are. She's gone, and you will never be able to torment her again. Rachel is out of your reach. Step out and let me show you how much I dislike you."

Tamara caught her breath. "Chloe? What are you doing? We don't challenge spirits." With my eyes closed and my head down, I formulated his image in my mind. I remembered how Rachel saw him. The leering grin on his face, his grasping hands. I captured the image perfectly and waved Tamara to silence. I couldn't explain to her what I was about to do. Time was not on my side. I was not going to be trapped in this place, not like Rachel had been for all these years with no justice.

Just in case, I looked at them both and said, "His name was Lee. He was her brother. He saw what happened. He came upon this incident after, and he didn't help her. She knew it. It was Lee." Kevin released another string of profanities, but at least they were quietly uttered swear words.

"Tamara, I need you to trust me. I'm going to lure him out of that spot, and I want you to step in it. You cannot argue with me about this. We don't have time. Step in the spot and cast a light."

"What color?"

"It doesn't matter! Pick one." She stepped into the spot, and I stepped back. I was happy to see that even though Carmichael heard everything I said, he didn't think I could do anything about it.

He didn't know I had a debt to pay.

He didn't know that I owed a soul.

"Come on, Carmichael. Hit me with your best shot!" Even as Tamara gasped at my challenge, the entity raced toward me. Clenching my fist, I bowed my head and closed my eyes. It didn't take but a second to make a connection with the Reaper. He was allowed to walk this property because they were connected, and he could have this one. No way would I show this guy the light. I was not his judge and jury, but I darn sure wasn't going to make this transition easy for Everett Carmichael Burns

Not in a hundred years.

I felt hard knuckles hit me in the gut, but it was only a momentary sensation. I endured it for Rachel.

For all the Rachels.

And the Annabels.

And the Annies.

The pain didn't last because the Reaper swirled into the yard on a cascade of dry leaves. He wrapped around Carmichael, and the unsuspecting man screamed. Unable to escape the Reaper's grasp, they both disappeared into the tree line beyond the house.

In silence, the three of us retreated to Kevin's truck, and none of us looked back. No one shed a tear or spoke for a long time. When we did, it wasn't about Rachel or Carmichael.

We talked about life things like pizza and sunshine and fishing. I really wanted to go fishing soon. I'd never caught a fish before. It was time to knock that off the list.

And maybe play some baseball.

"How about this? You build me a guest house, and Lynn can stay here in the main house. Otherwise, I'm going to have to relocate. I can't have that girl pining over me all the time. It's sad, and she knows I'm gay!" Joey was shuffling his cards in his hands as we sat at the kitchen table. He wanted to play Gin Rummy and was soundly beating me because I didn't have a clue about how to play the game. I was a quick learner, or so I had believed at first. My learning curve thrilled him to no end. At least he was momentarily happy about something.

It wouldn't last long because he was also frustrated with the new housing situation.

"Nope. I'm not building a guest house. I don't have the funds for that, and I refuse to use Chloe's trust fund for adding on to this place. Be sensible, Joey. I know that's hard, but try. You can move your room down here, where you can be closer to me. I'll keep her out of there. That's the best I can do."

Joey puffed on a cigarette that wasn't lit and placed it in the ashtray on the table. I had no idea where the cigarette or the ashtray had come from. Smoking was a new habit of his. He had picked it up because of his stress level, he said. I'd given Lynn instructions on how to make life better for Joey, but apparently, that wasn't enough. He wanted it to be just the three of us.

The sad truth was it would never be that. Chloe and I were living, and the living needed to change. Only the dead got to stay in one spot, never growing and never improving. The only thing they could do is move on to a better place.

I didn't have the heart to tell Joey that Chloe was going to college this fall out of state. It wasn't a permanent thing. This was her home, and she would come back to it eventually. I had my eye on a pretty little cottage in town. It was sad, now that everything was so peaceful here.

Chloe had every reason to return, and I knew she would, but she craved adventure, just like I had at her age. So had Tina Louise. So had Joey, although his attempts at adventure had led him to heartache and death.

That would not be Chloe's fate. I refused to let the fear of such things, the fear of those possibilities, influence her. I was dealing with feelings of loss and fear in my own way.

Joey was not the kind of person who welcomed change. He was the kind of guy who needed to keep things as they were, always and forever. Maybe it was a ghost thing, or maybe it was just a Joey thing. One could never tell.

"It's your turn, diva. Try not to make it too easy for me this hand." He arranged his cards carefully and tucked his bangs back into his Doo rag. This one was a white scarf with red cherries all over it. He was pretending he had put some sort of hair treatment on and was letting it sit. He'd also pretended that he painted his nails earlier. They were supposed to be a bright red, but his nails looked more black than anything. We did a lot of pretending, Joey and me. While it was comforting on some level, it wasn't good for me, and it wasn't good for him.

The inevitable loomed before us. We were dancing around it, and neither one of us wanted to talk about it. Joey was giving me an ultimatum about Lynn when the truth of the matter was this was about all of us, including him. His lingering at the Ridaught Plantation wasn't good for anyone. Chloe was finding her way in life. Lynn was finding peace with the past, and I had something great with Kevin.

I couldn't let that go. None of us could.

I studied my cards carefully before drawing one and discarding another. This was a poor hand. My shuffling skills had a lot to be desired. I sipped my cola and waited for Joey to make his move.

"What's the word on the killer? Is Lee really going to jail? I hate to say this, but I never heard of Rachel Burns before your investigation. I caught one of her movies the other night. She was genuinely talented in a Britney sort of way."

"I like Britney. I think she has tons of talent."

"I never took you for a Spears fan. More of a rocker. Maybe I have you all wrong, Tamara Garvey."

"He's going to jail. He didn't put up a fight. Kevin said

he wanted to talk about it. The sad thing is, he's sick. I mean, like bad-blood-disease sick. He won't live very long, but at least Rachel will have some sort of justice and is free."

Kevin had gone on a fishing trip with the girls. In a few weeks, we would be leaving for a lengthy road trip to Alabama. There were two reasons for the trip. One was to sign a new book contract, and the other was to visit the University of Alabama. Both the teens were interested in that particular college, and to my surprise, Chloe insisted on quietly paying for Lynn's tuition. Lynn didn't know about it, and if there was any way to keep it a secret, we were going to. Chloe was smart like her mother. She would do her best to help someone , but she wasn't going to be taken advantage of, and she didn't want Lynn to feel uncomfortable. Now that she had her focus back, Lynn was doing great in school and had proven to be an excellent student. It might be a bit of a challenge to raise her GPA, but there were summer courses that could help her look better on paper to the college of her choice. Chloe was encouraging her to apply for grants daily. One of those would come through for Lynn. Wink, wink. Nudge, nudge. Chloe would have it no other way.

As much as Chloe loved Lynn, and as deep as their friendship had grown, she was no fool. Best to keep friendships and money separate. In that, she was wise.

"Should've retired by the beach, not out here in the boonies of Louisiana." He puffed on his cigarette again, and I waited patiently for him to make his next move.

"You didn't retire, you died. Let's stop pretending, Joey. It is what it is."

He pressed his cards to his chest and peered at me over the edge of his horn-rimmed glasses. He must have raided the attic trunks to find those prizes. I didn't recognize them. Hopefully, they didn't belong to Lynn. He would definitely be sending the wrong signal if he was to begin sharing a wardrobe with her. Lynn was still infatuated with him. There was no doubt about that.

"Gee whiz, you're cranky. I liked you better when you were celibate. You were less sassy. If this is some sort of intervention, then just get to the point. I think it, you think it. We're all thinking it, but nobody is saying it!" He lifted his glasses slightly and dabbed at his eye as if he had an actual tear to shed.

"Okay, Svengali. What am I thinking, since you're such a mind reader?"

"You are thinking I should leave. You think it's time for me to move on. I think we all knew it was coming. What with Chloe working her mojo and moving people into the light all the time, and the Reaper hanging around looking like a forlorn hound dog. He still hangs out in the hallway once in a while. So creepy. I practically have to run from the shower to the bedroom on nights when there's a full moon. Doubly so now that I have a stalker living in my house. Yeah, I probably should go."

I pulled another card and pretended this was normal. That my heart was not breaking. That I didn't want to grab his ghostly hand and scream, "Never leave us!" That would be the selfish thing to do. I would only prove that I was treating him like a pet and not like a real friend. He accused me of that on occasion. I had laughed at first because it seemed so ridiculous, but he had it right all along. I didn't treat them like a pet, but definitely like a kid.

Joey wasn't that. He was a lost soul. He wasn't lost because he didn't know where to go, he knew that now. But there was a 5 foot, 4-inch-tall obstacle standing in his way.

"Where would you go? Would you cross over, or would you just relocate? Do you know what your options are?"

"Aren't you excited? I'm just thinking about it. I think I would rather relocate. Somewhere sunny, but then again, if I were to go to say, Panama Beach or even Biloxi, undoubtedly some weepy teenager would fall in love with me. I'm just too hot." He touched his chest with his finger and made a sizzling sound. It had been ages since I had seen anyone do that. I did not want to think about how many birthdays Joey had missed or whether he would have had kids by now.

"I can't let you become a haunted person, Tam. Not like Angela and Claude. What a sad pair those two are and continue to be. He's very dead, and she's almost dead. He's killing her, and I think he means it." He shuffled his pack of cigarettes and pulled out another one. That made a total of three in the ashtray. He didn't bother stabbing them out, but it wasn't like they were lit.

"I better warn her. I've been meaning to call her this week. I've had her on my mind. I liked her, but she's very standoffish. One of those people who lives in this world but belongs in another time."

Joey made a poor discard, and I snatched it up. "She knows, Tamara. She wants him to kill her. Angela believes that she killed him. It's this whole crazy story. I know I'm not supposed to eavesdrop, but sometimes I can't help it. When I knew you were bringing a curse-breaker into the place, I had to go check it out for myself. Besides, Linda and Robert got into this huge fight, and Linda came home early. She was too proud to come to get the dog, and I didn't want to be alone with her. That's a whole other thing."

"What?" I paused as I laid my card down with a slap.

He snapped his fingers in front of my eyes. "Try to keep up there, slowpoke. Anyway, I did what we do here. I did a little digging, a little investigating. I visited the hotel room. So sue me. It took a lot of energy to move so far away from home, but I managed it. I had to go dark for a while afterward, but I made it. I thought you'd be proud of me."

"Proud that you snooped on the curse-breaker? No. Why would I be?"

He gasped in surprise. "Oh no, you don't! You are just as snoopy as I am! Snoopier, if you ask me. They had this investigation, at least that's what Claude tells me. I'm not sure if I believe this guy. He has an error about him. You know, a superiority complex? It was a big thing in the 90s. Anyway, they had an investigation together. She couldn't go, so he went without her, yada yada. He got whacked with an axe."

"You lie! Where did you hear that story? Did Claude tell you that, or did you see it on television? On a paranormal show, perhaps?"

"O ye of little faith. I heard it from the horse's mouth! The girl they were trying to help, another cursed person, went completely nuts. Apparently, the curse was so severe that it allowed…no, that's not right. How did he put it? I can't remember. Something about making a portal for an evil spirit. It was attached to the curse, and when he broke it, this unseen thing boomeranged on him and…"

I leaned back in my chair and let out a hiss of air. "And yada yada. That's terrible. So, someone, he was trying to help attacked him? You think of this line of work as being scary but never deadly. I'll have to tell Chloe about this. She needs to be careful."

"What good would that do? Even Claude said it was a freak accident. He lived for a little while. He was in and out of his body quite a bit. Angela had to make a tough call. They pulled the respirator, and he was gone. She hates herself for it. I don't want that for you."

Studying my hand, I rearranged a few cards. Joey was keeping quiet to allow me to process all of this information. I had suspected that Claude was dead, but I didn't realize how messed up Angela's situation was. Now I was wondering how I could help her. I had no idea.

"I'm not ready for you to go." I didn't mean to blurt my confession like that, but there was no pulling it back. To my surprise, Joey didn't mock me or say something silly. He removed his glasses and put his cigarette down in the ashtray.

"I know, but we can't become Angela and Claude. It's not fair. You have a life to lead."

I didn't know what to say. I agreed with him, but my heart said otherwise. I waited for him to make his move, but luckily for me, I got another chance to draw a card. I finally won a hand! Not the game, but at least one hand. I could live with that.

"Read them and weep, Joey!" I spread the cards slowly, hoping he would notice the ring. He didn't at first, but then his eyes widened, and his newly replaced yet unlit cigarette fell out of his mouth.

Joey shrieked and clapped his hands. "Is that what I think it is? OMG! Look at that rock! Wait a second, how can he afford a ring like that? That's a monster! Is he a dirty cop, Tamara? He must be! How else could he afford a pricey diamond?"

"That's what you want to ask me? Not when did he pop the question, or how did it happen? I thought you were one for all the ooey-gooey details, Joey Lacoste. Don't you want a few of those?" I held my hand up and wiggled my fingers. He grabbed my hand, and I pretended that his cold skin didn't surprise me. I expected it, but it always shook me a little.

"Good score! Of course, I want to hear the details. I live for the details! Oh, my God! Does Chloe know? That little monster didn't say a word. I'm so tired of all the secrets around here. Why am I always the last to know everything?"

"She doesn't know yet. Kevin is going to tell her this weekend. We thought it would be a good idea for them to hang out some before… I mean, get to know each other." I cleared my throat as I began picking up the cards. Way to go, Tamara. Way to spill the beans and upset the apple cart.

"You can put your mind at ease. I know about Chloe and her plans. Those two blabbermouths can't keep a secret. They never shut up. I mean, they're constantly talking. It's like living with two myna birds up there. I just thought she would say something to me. Talk to me like she used to. She spends a lot of time pretending I'm not there. I know that's partly because of Lynn, but it hurts. A little."

He pulled the scarf off of his hair and plopped it down on the table, then leaned back in the chair and cocked his head as he studied me. He reminded me of a movie star, one who died back in the 1990s. His name was River something or other.

"How do you feel about that?" I packed the cards back in the worn box and closed it.

"Does it matter?"

It was my turn to study him. Joey's luminosity had faded a little during this conversation. He wasn't enjoying it, and neither was I, but we were doing the grownup thing and talking about it. That's what grown-ups do, right?

"Yes, it matters. To me. And to Chloe. You know what it's like being a young person. Life is endless. It's natural for a young person to want to spread their wings, Joey. We both have to let her go."

With a deep sigh and a flabbergasted expression, Joey said, "Subject change. On to the next, as Jason would say. Let's watch that Rachel Burns movie. You have it on Periscope, right? Can we play it on the big television? I'm dying to see the property. Too bad you couldn't record while Chloe was doing her thing. I would have loved to see that, but at least I can see inside the place. Really nice of the sheriff to allow you to walk through it again. I would never have the courage to go over there! You guys are so...so...

What's the word I'm looking for?" he asked as he trailed behind me into the living room.

"Uh, brave? Fearless?" I tapped on the device to put the video on the screen.

"I was thinking more like stupid, but let's go with fearless. I mean, you go looking for trouble like you don't have any street smarts. How did you make it as a stripper? Oh, excuse me, burlesque entertainer. Hey! That would be a totally cool theme for a wedding, like a burlesque theater!"

"Shut your mouth! No, hell no. Get that out of your head, and for your information, Kevin knows all about it. I can't say the sheriff does, but I don't guess that matters. He's retiring next month. I think Kevin is going to be moving up. I hope so. I think he wants it."

"Interesting. The new sheriff and a woman with a shady past..."

"He's cool with it, and so am I. I did what I had to do to get by, okay? We were all hustling back in the day." I flopped on the couch as Joey grinned at me. "You were kidding, right?"

"Yes, I was kidding, but you should have seen the look on your face. And honey child, Kevin looks great with a tan." He swatted his face with his hand as if he were having a hot flash. As always, Joey was careful not to speak too flirtatiously about my guy. It was kind of a thing we did. We had *some* boundaries.

"Hey, those skinny jeans look great on you, Tam."

"Thanks." I smiled sweetly.

"Just kidding. Don't wear those again. Those should go to Goodwill. How soon until the wedding? Do we have time to drop a few pounds? Oh, no! This isn't a shotgun wedding, is it?" He eyed my stomach suspiciously as I denied any such situation.

"I don't think that's funny. I'm as trim as ever." I pouted as I clutched the pillow and held it over my stomach to camouflage myself. Joey tilted his head down and pursed his lips at me. "See, I do need you, Joey Lacoste. I need you around to help me with this wedding. I'm not ready for you to go. That's the truth. How could I possibly do all this without you? At least stay until the wedding. Then you can pack your bags and move to Aruba if you want, and I won't complain."

"So needy, Tamara. Fine. Until the wedding, then it's *adios*. Hey, is Aruba in Mexico? Never mind, that's probably too hot, and I can't speak Spanish."

Joey was joking, of course. He couldn't leave this place for long. He'd just confessed as much to me. "You've got time to figure it out. It's going to be a summer wedding. Only three months away."

Joey whistled and whispered, "Are you sure this is not a shotgun type of deal? What's the rush? These things take time, Tamara. Lots of time. You'll have a challenge finding a venue so close to the date."

"We're having it here. This is the perfect venue, don't you think? Absolutely perfect. It's the place that brought us all together."

"Perfect if slasher film is your theme."

"Come on, that's not fair. Beautiful things have happened here. I want to have this wedding before Chloe leaves. I want us all together. Here, with all the ghosts."

"Okay, but I can at least do your hair. I know the perfect

updo. A little sparkle, a little dab of something. Slick this side and poof that one. Oh, yes. I know just the thing!"

I paused the video. He wasn't watching it, and I did think my behind was far too big on the screen. I could at least drop five pounds. That I could do.

"No. You aren't doing my hair."

"Pick out the dress? Select the cake? What's my job? I know perfectly well you are too much of a control freak to let me be your wedding planner."

"You are right about that. You know me too well. I'm the wedding planner. We're going simple but classic." I leaned my head on the back of the couch, feeling grateful for this moment. For this weird friendship that I would forever treasure, no matter where life took me.

Joey crossed his arms across his chest and blew through his lips. "Then what am I doing here? You want me to stick around for the wedding, but I have no part in it? That's not cool. You're killing me, Tamara. Literally killing me."

I didn't take advantage of his incorrect use of the word literally. I wanted this moment to be a good one. One I would always remember. Hopefully, he would too. "I want you to give me away, Joey."

"What?" Joey's face grew even brighter. His smile tugged at my heart, and I felt his joy. "You want me to give you away? Really? I can walk with you?" I nodded, not caring how it sounded. If he could muster the strength to walk me down the aisle, I would welcome his arm. I would embrace it.

"I can't ask you to be my maid of honor; that has to be Chloe. But I want you to walk with me, Joey Lacoste."

He wiped his eyes and nodded. "Of course, I will. I will be glad to do it. Can I wear a tux?"

"Yep. Even one with rhinestones, but no dress. There's only one bride walking down that aisle." I squeezed his cold hand and quickly released it.

He pouted but grinned. "You know me so well. It's going to be the most fabulous yet simple wedding Crystal Springs has ever seen. You won't regret this, Tamara. I love you."

"I love you too, Joey."

"No popcorn for you. You'll have to lay off the sweets. Do you have a bridal book yet? No? We need to order one. Get the computer! Never mind, let's just go to your office. We have a wedding to plan!"

I watched Joey sail out the door and heard my office door creak open. It was weird not hearing the footsteps in between, but that was life with Joey. I was going to miss him when he moved on, and he would. He had to, as did I.

"What are you waiting on, an engraved invitation?" Joey hollered at me from the office down the hall. "That's number one! We need those too!"

"What?"

I could hear my computer dinging as he turned it on. Oh, shoot. I hope he didn't burn that one up too. Ghosts and hard drives did not play well together.

"Nothing. On the way."

I reached for a few mints from the vintage glass bowl I kept on the coffee table.

"Don't even think about it. Drop the sugar, Tamara."

"Yes, Officer. On the way. I swear, I need to put a bell on you." I dropped the candy and got off the couch to begin what promised to be an hour-long shopping spree courtesy of some online bridal store.

I had a good life, and it was exactly as I wanted it: a curse free, Joey-filled, hard loving life.

And it was all mine.

The End

AUTHOR'S NOTE

Hey, everyone! I had a great time writing the third book in the *Welcome to Dead House* Series. What a wild ride! From crashing chandeliers to the dead knocking on the front door, it has been a hoot hanging out at the Ridaught Plantation. Exploring myths and legends of the South is something I love to do, and implementing them into my stories is exciting. I love storytelling, and it does my heart good to keep these legends and ghostly tales alive, even if only through my fiction. When I get to have these adventures alongside characters like Tamara Garvey and Chloe Carol, it's even more exciting!

The Dead House might remind you of a house you know. Maybe. Maybe not. It is certainly based on a few of them I've visited in Louisiana, namely Oak Alley and the Myrtles Plantation.

Personally, I think every community, parish, and county down here has an old home like the Ridaught Plantation, or even a haunted post office. (I have visited a few.) Places that remain abandoned and are potential storehouses of gruesome secrets have always fascinated the curious. (Also me.) Maybe you remember wondering about such a place when you were a kid? Being the curious sort, I was always fascinated with those odd spots. Sometimes the unfortunate in our society, the homeless, were forced to call these places home, at least for the night. You wouldn't believe some of the things they have experienced. Talk about the stuff of nightmares.

In Tamara's case, the Ridaught Plantation continues to offer a place for future memories to be born and recorded and maybe one day revisited. Her fictional community is equally fascinated and terrified of the house because of its notorious history.

My fascination for haunted houses began at a very early age. If you've been on this writing journey with me for any length of time, you know all about my experiences in haunted Ohio. I have shared about it extensively on my blog. We have our spooks down here in the South, but to my mind, the things I experienced in Ohio, namely Perry County, are far spookier than any *boogaloo* we could ever drum up down here.

Maybe one day I will write a story about my own haunted house experiences. Until then, I'll continue to dream up places for you and me to safely visit. As I was writing this book, my mind naturally went to other stories I've written. You may have picked up the *Seven Sisters* series or *Idlewood* or *Sugar Hill*. In all of those, I took readers to haunted locations that were the homes of tragic characters, most of whom were seeking justice in life and in death.

The *Dead House* books were quite a bit different for me to write because although Chloe and Tamara both have dream experiences, they are not dream-catchers. Not like Carrie Jo, who is the central character for the *Seven Sisters* books. But Chloe's psychic abilities fascinate me. (What about y'all? Any psychics out there?)

The study of curses and curse-breaking is a new field of interest for me, so it was fun to explore it on behalf of Angela Webster. For any of you that actually work in unraveling curses, here's a hat tip to you. Wow! What a deeply spiritual and frightening field of work! I'll stick to writing about them, not trying to break them. I hope I did a decent job describing those very complicated processes, and I am completely aware that my knowledge is limited in scope. Please forgive me if I missed a few things for the sake of better entertainment.

For Chloe, the future is bright.

The possibilities are endless for Tina Louise's daughter. I can see her going to college and becoming an amazing Egyptologist or maybe a travel blogger with a huge following. Just like Betsy would have been had she lived. Anything is possible for that independent young woman.

I like that Chloe, despite her challenges with her family and the loss of her mother, did not become a boy-crazy teenager. Chloe is an independent thinker in all things, and who else would have been strong enough in her family to have fought through such a horrible curse so successfully? I wish I had been more like Chloe Carol growing up. I think we'll see more of her in the future, and again, I believe that future is going to be a bright one.

As far as Tamara goes, she will find happiness in her own time and in her own way. Despite whatever she might say, Tamara wants the white picket fence experience and her 2.5 children, and now that can happen. She's been the girl who's had her hands in both worlds but has her feet firmly planted in this reality. Once her task is done, once Chloe no longer needs her, I suspect Tamara will probably leave the paranormal behind for good, not for any other reason except so that she can have both arms open to embrace her future. Tamara is learning that her mind is just as beautiful as the rest of her and that she has so much more to offer than what people may first believe. I suspect that Tam and Kevin will buy a place in the country together and have a happy life. Who knows?

Joey, however, is my wildcard. I don't know about you, but Joey reminds me a bit of Peter Pan, the boy who never wanted to grow up. The one time he tried the grown-up thing, he got it wrong. Joey is a beautiful soul who was never understood in life and desperately wants that before crossing over for good.

I toyed with the idea of bringing us all into the moment when Joey forgave Aaron, but I decided against it for now. The main reason was that I wanted to give him some privacy, and I felt as if that conversation was one we can eavesdrop on in the future if we return to the Dead House.

Anything is possible, but I guess like all book or television series, the future is in your hands.

How do you feel about Tamara and Chloe? What about Joey? Do you want to continue reading and explore their storylines with me? I'd love to hear from you to get your opinions. I want to write what you want to read. While I'm pounding away on the keyboard, I always have you in mind. Deep in my soul, at the barest foundation of who I am, I am a storyteller—your storyteller. But if I'm the only one sitting around the fire and no one is listening, I'm just a gal hanging out by the fire.

That's not quite what I have in mind.

So what do you think? Drop me a line and let me know. Email me at authormlbullock@gmail.com or contact me through Facebook. I also have a website, MLBullock.com where you can reach me.

Very soon, I will have written one hundred books. Wouldn't it be cool if that one-hundredth book was a *Welcome to Dead House* installment? I think so.

Until we speak again, stay spooky.

All my best,
M.L. Bullock

Want to be notified when my next book releases? Click here.

Want to follow me on social media and see my writing progress? Eager to get peeks of my daily life, and my embarrassingly extensive planner collection? I have you covered.

Follow me here: Facebook - Twitter – Instagram – Website

The Seven Sisters Ultimate Cottonwood Saga, including two bonus stories.

When historian Carrie Jo Jardine accepted her dream job as the chief historian at Seven Sisters in Mobile, Alabama, she had no idea what she would encounter.

The moldering old plantation housed more than a few boxes of antebellum artifacts and forgotten oil paintings.

Secrets lived there--and they demanded to be set free.

When young, wealthy Ashland Stuart offered Carrie Jo the job, he had no idea that she had a secret of her own.

An unexpected accident takes Carrie Jo back in time as a witness to life at the plantation over 150 years ago.

An impassioned plea from Ashland puts Carrie Jo in a precarious position as the two work together to find young and beautiful missing heiress Calpurnia Cottonwood.

A collection of journals and a series of dreams give Carrie Jo all the clues she needs to find the missing girl, but both a present-day danger and one from the past try to stop her.

Will Carrie Jo solve the mystery of the house *or will she go missing forever herself?*

Grab your copy today!

MEET THE AUTHOR

Author of the best-selling *Seven Sisters* series and the *Gulf Coast Paranormal* series, M.L. Bullock has been storytelling since she was a child. A student of archaeology, she loves weaving stories that feature local Alabama legends. She currently lives on the Gulf Coast with her family but frequently travels to explore the southern states she loves so much. When she's not writing, she enjoys the odd paranormal investigation. The odder, the better.

Connect with M.L. Bullock on Facebook. To receive updates on her latest releases, visit her website at M.L. Bullock and subscribe to her mailing list. You can also contact her at authormlbullock@gmail.com.

Seven Sisters: The Cottonwood Saga

The Idlewood Collection: The Complete Idlewood Series

Beyond Seven Sisters

The Desert Queen Collection: The Complete Series

The Hauntings of Sugar Hill

Lost Camelot

Shabby Hearts

www.ingramcontent.com/pod-product-compliance
Lightning Source LLC
Chambersburg PA
CBHW050302110726

47898CB00007B/2502